DRUM

DRUM

WILL OVERBY

DAWSON SPRINGS, KENTUCKY
2012

This is a work of fiction. Names, characters, businesses, places, events and incidents are either the products of the author's imagination or used in a fictitious manner. Any resemblance to actual persons, living or dead, or actual events is purely coincidental.

ISBN-13: 978-0615692746
ISBN-10: 0615692745

ONE

1

Ham pulls the Escalade into the driveway and cuts off the engine. He sits in the dark warmth of the car and looks through the dining room windows of the house. Inside, he can see Christina in the kitchen cooking something on the stove. She is wearing a light blue apron, and her dark hair (streaked with strands of gray that drive him crazy with desire) is pulled back off her face. It's good to be home, he thinks.

He steps out of the car, grabbing his briefcase and pulling his topcoat around him against the sharp November wind. The late autumn depresses him. When the time changes, darkness descends around four-thirty, the time he usually gets home from the bank. He glances at the dying glow of the sun in the west, remembering. This was the time of year when Jill died.

Inside the front door, he sets his case on the floor and piles his coat on top of it. "I'm home," he calls. Christina has spread his mail on the chest in the foyer;

he glances at it, then heads on into the house. Christina is still at the stove, her back to him. "I'm home," he says again.

She turns and gives him a smile. "'Bout time," she says. "Dinner's almost ready."

He goes up behind her and runs his arms around her waist, kissing her on the neck. "What're we having?" he asks.

"You're cold," she says, her face pressing against his. She stirs the vegetables in the skillet. "I'm fixing broiled flounder and California veggies."

He sniffs the air. "Smells good."

"Kipp called," Christina says. "He had basketball practice." She glances at the clock. "He ought to be home any minute."

As if on cue, the front door bangs shut and Kipp ambles in from the front hall. His hair hangs down on his forehead in a sweaty mop, and his glasses have begun to steam up. His red and white letter jacket hangs open, revealing his wrinkled Oak Heights Academy T-shirt. "Hey," he says.

"You're gonna get sick," Ham says, "running around in the cold like that."

Kipp turns back, heading for his room. "Aw, Dad."

Ham follows him. "How'd practice go?"

Kipp shuffles down the hall and into his room, shedding his jacket. "All right." He turns on the light, revealing piles of papers, compact discs, clothes and books. He throws his jacket on the unmade bed and pulls out of his shirt. Ham notices how the boy has muscled up in the past year, how his chest and arms have begun to fill out. "I made an A on my algebra test," Kipp says, unbuckling his jeans.

"Terrific." Ham steps around the corner into his own bedroom. "Dinner's about ready," he calls to Kipp.

* * *

Ham was once married to Jill. He met her at college where they were both in a political science class. That was the fall of his senior year, and after graduation they were married. Six years later, Kipp was born, and fourteen years after that, Jill died. Ovarian cancer. She didn't know until it had spread all through her.

Ham and Christina have been together now for a year. Sometimes in the musky afterglow of their lovemaking, when Christina is breathing softly the rhythm of sleep, Ham lies awake staring at the ceiling, wondering what Jill would think of Christina. The guilt still washes over him, even though Jill has been dead two years.

Ham hangs up his suit and tie and tosses his T-shirt into the clothes hamper. In his bathroom, standing before the mirror in his silk boxers, he examines his body, running his fingertips over his slack belly and sagging pectorals. "God," he says; even the hair on his chest is turning gray. He gives his reflection a silly grin and pulls on a ragged pair of Levi's and an old blue oxford.

"I'll be out in the shop," he says to Christina as he passes through the kitchen.

"Don't be too long; this fish'll be like rubber if it gets cold."

"I just want to see how the chest looks." He steps down into the biting chill of the garage and eyes his latest restoration project. The bureau came from the attic of his father's house. Ham chipped and sanded through layers of dense, dark paint to reach the solid oak beneath. Last night he gave it a final coat of polyurethane, and now he runs his hand over the top, impressed at the smooth, glass-like finish.

"Dad?"

Ham jumps at Kipp's voice, then smiles. "C'mere. Look at this."

Kipp steps down and gazes at where his father is pointing. "Looks good."

"Feel how smooth this surface is."

Kipp strokes the top and smiles. "You did good."

Ham reaches down and wads up the newspaper he has spread over the floor. "I don't know where Christina wants to put it. My bedroom, I guess."

Kipp is pointing at the balled-up paper in Ham's hands. "Remember, don't throw that away. Put it in the recycling bin."

"I forgot." He steps over to the stack inside. "When are you taking this stuff out of here, anyway? I never saw such a mess of cans and bottles and shit."

"I'm working down at the center Saturday afternoon, so I'll take it then. Dad, I—"

"It's not that I'm anti-environmental or anything," Ham is saying. "I just get tired of walking around this crap."

Kipp nods. "I know. Listen, Dad. . . "

Ham looks up. "Yeah?"

Kipp shoves his hands into the pockets of his jeans. "I don't wanna go tomorrow."

Ham blinks. "Oh. All right."

Tomorrow is the anniversary of Jill's death. Last

year the two of them took flowers to her grave. "I know you really want me to," he tells his father, "but I just don't feel like it."

"No problem."

"Will Christina go with you?"

"I don't know." Truthfully, Ham hadn't thought of asking Christina. In fact, he doesn't even know what she thinks of it. He looks up at Kipp's pained expression and smiles. "It's all right. You don't have to go if you don't want to."

"You won't be disappointed?"

"No. It's all right."

Kipp smiles and steps back up into the house. Ham leans back against his workbench, his thumbs tucked through his belt loops; the shine on the chest looks good, he thinks.

* * *

Christina has loaded the dishwasher and now is wiping off the table. Ham sits at the bar, watching her, sipping on his second beer. "Dinner was great," he tells her.

"Tell me something."

"Anything."

"Whatever happened to our rule that when one of us cooks, the other cleans up?"

"When did we decide that?"

"Last spring."

"We did?"

She rolls her eyes. "It was your idea. You said you hated to see me do all the work every night."

"I did?"

She nods, then swipes his nose with the dishcloth as she passes him.

Ham drains the rest of his beer and crunches the can in his fist. "Where're we putting our cans now?"

"Pantry," Christina tells him. "Brown paper bag."

Ham scrounges through the brooms and mops until he finds the bag on the floor. Just as he tosses the can, his gaze lights upon a souvenir glass from Beale Street. A pang of grief hits his stomach; the Memphis trip was the last he and Jill took together. Just before she became ill.

"I think it's great the school's operating that recycling center," Christina is saying. "I think it'll teach the kids a lot."

Ham stands with his hand still clutching the pantry doorknob. "I think Kipp's turning into an environmental nut," he says. His vision blurs and he realizes tears are welling up in his eyes. He blinks them back quickly; God, Christina will think he's crazy.

Kipp pops into the room, grinning. "I heard that." He slaps Ham on the shoulder. "I'm going over to Amber's."

"Okay."

"I may be late," he says, heading for the front door.

"Not too late," Ham calls after him. "Remember school tomorrow."

Ham stands like a stone until he hears Kipp's car roar off down the street, then shuts the door and turns to Christina. "I need to talk to you about something."

Christina starts the dishwasher. "Would you drink some decaf?"

Ham takes hold of her shoulders and turns her around. She looks into his eyes. "Ham, what's wrong? You're crying."

He pulls her close, pressing his face into her hair.

Tears are spilling freely down his cheeks now. "Why can't I get over her?" he whispers.

She wraps her arms around him. "Jill?"

He nods. "It's been two years. Two years tomorrow. Why can't I get over it? Am I just crazy?"

She pulls back and kisses him. "No, baby. You're not crazy. It just takes time."

"But two years. . ."

"It takes some people longer than others."

He runs his nose along his sleeve. "Will you do something for me? Will you go with me to the cemetery tomorrow?"

"If you want me to."

"I need you with me."

She pulls him back to her. "I'll go."

He kisses her neck. "I love you."

2

In the warmth of Ham's bed, snuggled against his chest, Christina lies watching the light of the passing traffic play on the walls. She listens to his steady breathing, knowing he is asleep, wondering if he is dreaming. Smoothing his hair with her fingers, she feels a rush of love so strong it seems caught in her throat, and her eyes fill with tears. Sometimes when they make love, like tonight, Ham's sadness touches her so deeply and so strongly that it seems as if she is holding onto a bundle of hurt. She wants to clutch him against her breast and let him cry until all the grief, the bitterness, is spent, until his sadness is withered and dry as a stone.

Now, as she rests in the crook of his arm, she feels his seed trickling from her, the product of their love, and she thinks maybe she can sense sadness in that as well.

When Christina was twenty-three she married a man named Kevin. Kevin was wild; it was the eighties, so they smoked a little pot, drank a ton of wine coolers, and took a lot of trips on Kevin's motorcycle. After they had been together a year, Kevin began snorting coke. Then the fights began, arguments over money and bills mostly. Christina knew most of Kevin's paycheck was going up his nose, and she confronted him with it. Then one night he slapped her with the back of his hand and her cheek swelled into a purple blob. She left him the next day and went to her mother's. Soon after, he started calling, crying, telling her he was turning their life together into shit, that she was just throwing away the past couple of years. He showed up on the doorstep one morning about three-thirty; her father met him with a shotgun and told him he didn't ever want to see his ass again or he'd blow him to hell and back. Kevin left town not long after they divorced, and she hasn't heard from him since. And that's just how she wants it.

Eventually, Christina returned to college and earned her bachelor's in business. Then she received her real estate license, and after several years she started her own agency. It was at that time, when she went to the bank to apply for a business loan, that she met the vice president of First State Bank, Hamilton Bradford, Jr. He was her loan officer, and after he had given her the money and she had opened her office, he dropped by a couple of times to see how things were going. She learned that he was a widower with a teenage son, that he enjoyed French wines and golf and

Italian food. On one of his visits he invited him to her apartment for dinner—her lasagna—and he accepted.

That was a little over a year ago. And now here she lies, one leg draped across his hips, her fingers playing over his chest, and in some ways she still feels as though he has presented her with nothing but a blank wall. Part of her resents the fact that he still mourns a woman who has been dead two years; that he has refused to accept her death and move on with his life. But that is part of the mystery of him, part of the canvas he has yet to unveil.

She kisses his ear. "Ham, wake up."

"Hhmm?"

"I need to go. Before Kipp gets home."

He stirs, wrapping his arms around her and kissing her lips. "Do you have to?"

"I need to." She kisses him once more and pulls away, stepping out into the cold room to dress in the dark. "I'll call you at work tomorrow," she says. "You can let me know what time you want to go to the cemetery."

"Okay."

She pauses in the bedroom door and looks back at his shape beneath the cover. "I love you," he says, and his voice is thick with sleep.

3

Kipp pulls his black Mazda 3 out of Amber's driveway, heading toward home. They have been dating since the beginning of the school year; this is longest Kipp has been with anyone, and he realizes he may need to move on to someone else soon. He knows Amber thinks she is in love with him; he is not sure what he feels. They have had a few bad fights and even broken up once, but they have finally settled into a rhythm that is comfortable. The complacency is what disturbs Kipp; there is no excitement, no discovery anymore.

They have made love twice, both times in Kipp's bed while his dad and Christina were out. Amber is Kipp's first lover, and the fact that she has been with other guys before him is another thing that bothers him. He knows she is not a slut, but something about the whole situation just doesn't seem right.

Kipp pops in an Anthrax CD and turns up the volume until he can feel the pulse of the sub-woofer in his balls. Loud music has never failed to give him an erection, something he feels guilty about and cannot explain. He has never told anyone this, especially Amber.

As he turns onto the boulevard, he catches sight of Christina's car turning off toward her street. He wonders about Ham and Christina, if they will ever marry. They sleep together sometimes, he knows. He has learned this from doing the laundry. Even though Ham tries to conceal it, Kipp knows you can't hide your sex life from the person who washes your sheets. Christina doesn't stay overnight, even though he is certain she does when he is not home. Kipp would like to just say to Ham, "Hey, I know you two sleep together, and it's okay. She can stay over if she wants." But his father would probably shit a brick.

Kipp pulls into a convenience store and fills his car with gas, then eases up into a parking space. He has just slid his wallet from his back pocket when he looks up to see the clerk behind the counter, and he is jolted as he realizes it is his Uncle Bruce.

He knows his father's brother has served seven years in prison, but that's about all. Ham never discusses Bruce, and Kipp never asks about him. It's as if Bruce has ceased to exist, that he is as dead as Kipp's mother.

Now, heart pounding, Kipp stands outside the store, his wallet in his hands, not knowing what to do or say. He slips through the door and glances around; there are no other customers. He inches his way toward the register, examining his uncle.

Bruce has not looked up. He is counting out dollar bills and clipping them into groups of twenty-five. His hair is dark and receding, and his nose juts out hawkishly from beneath heavy eyebrows. Through the blue uniform, Kipp can see that Bruce is stocky, fat. Funny, he thinks; he looks nothing like Ham.

"Thirty dollars," Bruce says, not looking at him.

Kipp slides the money across the counter, his gaze level.

Bruce takes it and gives him a quick smile. Kipp thinks he sees a slight glimmer of recognition in Bruce's expression, but then it is gone. "Thank you," Bruce tells him. "Come back."

Kipp heads for the door, walking on his toes as if he is afraid of making a sound. He doesn't know if Bruce knows him or not, and he is too afraid to say anything. As he slips into his car, he realizes he has been holding his breath since he went inside.

Back at home, he shivers in the night air as he struggles with his key, trying to unlock the door without making any noise. Moving through the dark house, he barks his shin on the chest in the foyer. "Shit."

"That you, Kipp?" his father calls.

"Yeah, Dad." Shit, he thinks again. He stops at Ham's door, peering in at the darkness. "Sorry if I woke you."

"'S all right. You have a good time?"

"Yeah."

"G'night."

"'Night." Kipp remains motionless for a moment, thinking about his father and his uncle, wondering if Ham knows Bruce is working at a Gas-N-Pack across town. He thinks about Christina slipping beneath the green light on the boulevard in her white BMW, then wonders if his father is naked beneath his sheets. He turns away, disgusted with himself.

He remembers telling Ham he doesn't want to go to the cemetery tomorrow, and guilt stabs at his stomach. It seems senseless, though; two years of grieving won't bring his mother back. Last year at this time Ham went into a deep depression, and Kipp dreads the next few days. He hopes Christina will go with Ham to the cemetery, because at least then his father won't be alone.

4

Bruce glances at the clock for the third time in an hour. Three-thirty. Outside, the store lot is empty, as it has been since midnight. Nights like these are agonizing. He has already stocked the shelves, swept the floors, straightened the food bar and clipped his money for his bank deposit. Six o'clock is still an eternity away.

Earlier, just as he came on his shift, he thinks Ham's son was in, but he is not sure. He hasn't seen

Kipp in several years, and he doesn't remember the boy wearing glasses. But then Bruce hasn't even talked to Ham since their mother died fifteen years ago. And that was just after Bruce entered prison.

He still remembers being called into the visitation room and seeing Ham behind the desk—Ham in his Hart, Marx and Schaffner suit and his Italian silk tie and his white Ralph Lauren shirt. And as Bruce sank into the chair opposite his brother, Ham said, "Our mother's dead. She had a stroke." He stared at the desktop as he said it, his gaze not meeting Bruce's. And even as Bruce sobbed like a child, Ham only stared at him, his expression stern and accusing. But the worst part was being taken to the funeral home by two armed guards and having to walk in handcuffed and shackled and stand before his mother's casket like a murderer, then be taken back to the penitentiary without attending the service. And on the way out, he passed his father and Ham sitting with Jill and Kipp, who was just a year old. Only Jill looked at him and gave him a sympathetic half-smile. And that was the last time Bruce saw his family; his card to Ham when Jill died went unacknowledged.

Bruce knows that his conviction hurt his father's and brother's careers—that was made clear to him. In all the newspaper clippings of his case Bruce collected, he is always referred to as "the son of Bradford Industries owner Hamilton Bradford and brother of First State Bank executive Hamilton Bradford, Jr." In fact, when his father sold the company for several million dollars a few years ago, the media still made vague references to Bruce.

Bruce thinks of that money with bitter revulsion.

All while he was growing up there were never any financial worries. Bradford Industries was a thriving company, a maker of machine parts, and his father had made good business and investment decisions over the years. And since his brother was nearly ten years older than he, Bruce practically lived as an only child, affluent and privileged. But now he struggles by, making just above minimum wage after eight years at the Gas-N-Pack. He thinks about that money, and anger burns like hot coals in his belly.

His senior year in college, Bruce went out with a girl named Pamela Myers. After their date, they went back to her room. They had both been drinking heavily. Sloppily and drunkenly, they fumbled with each other, kissing and fondling until Pamela passed out. Bruce somehow managed to make his way back to his apartment, where he fell asleep on the bathroom floor. The next morning, when he was groggy and nauseated with the aftereffects, when he had just been awake enough to realize he had thrown up all over himself sometime during the night, two cops showed up at his door to arrest him on a charge of rape. Pamela had called them and told them he had forced her to have sex. It didn't seem to matter how much Bruce had protested, how much he tried to convince everyone what had really happened. The case went to trial, and even his father's attorney was unable to save Bruce from a ten-year sentence, of which he served seven.

Bruce is disturbed most by his family's abandonment of him. He feels alone and adrift. It's as if the family's feelings for him died with his mother. She was the only woman he ever admired, the only one who ever gave a damn about him. The only one who truly seemed to believe his story. And the vision of Ham sitting down to tell him of her death still swims before him, the expression on Ham's face that screamed, "Our mother is dead, and you killed her." He supposes that his conviction might have had some indirect influence on her stroke, but goddammit! He would just like to take Ham by the shoulders and shake him senseless and say, "Wake up, you stupid son-of-a-bitch!"

Bruce tears his nametag from his smock and throws it on the counter. He was at least able to get this job through a special reformatory program after the manager looked at his college records. Bruce had been majoring in finance when he was arrested, and his high grades in economics impressed even the owner of the Gas-N-Pack chain. But none of that means any more money in his wallet. He is an ex-con and always will be. He has entertained the idea of finishing up his bachelor's, but he knows that financially he will never be able; colleges aren't exactly willing to fork over financial aid to a convicted rapist.

He stares out the dusty windows at the lot with its flood-lit gas pumps and huge blue-and-white GAS-N-PACK sign. The clouds that have hung over town all day have finally opened, and rain begins to pelt the concrete.

TWO

1

Ham sits in the quiet of the living room, watching the sky turn pink above the back yard. The patio is wet from the overnight rain. He laces his fingers around the warmth of his coffee cup. Jill has been dead two years today.

The empty pain that still gnaws in his gut brings with it pangs of guilt. He hates himself for asking Christina to go to the cemetery with him; he knows she wants to — for him — and that's what fuels his shame. How can he expect the woman who loves him so unconditionally to placate him by visiting the grave of another woman, the woman he still mourns?

Work will not go well today. He has several loan customers to interview, and the president will expect Ham's bank income statement to be completed by noon. But somehow he will leave early, even if that means he must cancel some appointments.

Ham has been with the bank now for over twenty-five years. Just out of college he accepted a teller position; the salary was six hundred dollars a month, and he smiles about that now. But the top management was impressed with his enthusiasm and his innovative ideas, and eighteen months later he was a branch manager making twenty thousand a year. Ham ran that branch until about five years ago, when he was promoted to senior vice president. And now it seems as though there is no other place to go, nothing else to work toward. He would like to keep moving up; he thinks often about becoming bank president someday, but at his age it doesn't look as though that will happen. The man who is president now is younger than Ham, and Ham sometimes wonders how different his career might have been if his brother had not been convicted of rape. But that is a dead-end question.

Ham squints to read the clock in the kitchen and sets his empty cup on the coffee table. It's time to wake up Kipp.

He pads barefoot to the boy's room and knocks softly on the closed door, then eases inside. Kipp is covered from head to toe with his down comforter, a shapeless blob in the faint light. Ham touches his son's shoulder and turns on the bedside lamp. "Kipp, it's seven o'clock." He pulls the cover down and Kipp's face screws up tight in the sudden light.

Kipp rolls over, his back to the lamp. "Okay."

Ham watches him for a moment, remembering how when Kipp was small Ham would stand over his bed at night, looking at him, afraid to leave his side lest he stop breathing. A rush of love washes over him, and he reaches out to stroke Kipp's hair. "Come on," he says, "you need to get up."

Kipp blows out a breath. "Okay."

* * *

Ham's father lives in a modest home in Old Town, that section of the city where the established families have long maintained their restored Victorian houses and proudly displayed their wealth. But Hamilton Senior has lived in the same simple frame house for over fifty years, and no one would suspect it is the home of a millionaire.

Ham steps inside, the screen door banging behind him, and the empty kitchen greets him with the smells of coffee and bacon. "Dad?"

His father shuffles in, thin and pale, one hand on the wall for support. "Morning."

Ham is suddenly afraid. His father looks so old this morning. His white hair is splayed over his head in unruly tufts, and his pajamas droop over his bony frame like a shroud. He notices with horror that his father's penis lolls through his unbuttoned fly. "Dad, you. . . " He points.

Hamilton Senior peers down at his crotch and reddens. "Oh." He fumbles with the tiny snaps on the pajama bottoms. "Sorry."

As his father plops down at the table, Ham pours them each a cup of coffee. "How are you this morning?"

Hamilton Senior runs a hand over his hair. "Kinda dizzy."

"You take your blood pressure medicine?"

"Yeah. Yeah, I took that first thing when I got up." He takes a sip of coffee. "Just feel. . . weak. Weak as a cat."

Ham looks at his father's hands, watching as the pink, blotchy fingers grasp the coffee cup. Arms that Ham remembers being strong and beefy now seem wilted, the skin thin and translucent. The fear burns in his stomach again; it's as though he has not really seen his father in years, as though what he has been looking at was not a real man but a projection of emotions and thoughts.

He glances at his watch. "I guess I need to go."

His father looks up. "Will you put some salve on me before you leave?"

Ham nods and steps into his father's bedroom for the green jar of Vick's Vap-O-Rub. "Kipp's got a ball game tomorrow night," he says as the odor of the salve stabs through his nose and into his eyes. "I wish you'd go with us."

"I'll see how I feel." His father is unbuttoning his pajama top. His chest is thin and bony, and the nipples sag like the breasts of an old woman. "This weather's so dry I can hardly get my breath."

Ham rubs the medicine across his father's chest, amazed at how large his hand seems against his father's body, at how clearly the ribs stand out. "Dad, are you eating all right?"

"Yeah. Fine."

"You seem kinda thin."

His father smiles. "Been eating like a horse. Had bacon and eggs this morning. Baked a can of biscuits, too."

Ham screws the lid onto the jar and washes his hands in the kitchen sink. "I don't like that dizziness you had this morning. I'll make an appointment with the doctor for you."

"No. I'm okay. I don't need to see the doctor."

Ham sighs impatiently. "Dad, you're losing weight. You're dizzy. You can't get your breath. It won't hurt to check it out with Dr. Steinfield. Then if it's nothing at least we'll know."

Hamilton Senior nods, pulling his top back on. "You're right. You're a good son, Bruce."

Ham reels as if from a slap. He knows his father is unaware of what he has said. The fear has settled into Ham's stomach again and along with it, hurt.

2

The sun is bright and hot as Ham and Christina pull into the cemetery. Ham has not spoken since he picked her up, and Christina is beginning to wonder if her coming with him was a good idea. His forehead is wrinkled and his eyebrows have that slight downward cast they assume when he is not feeling well. She reaches out and grasps his leg. "Ham, are you all right?"

He nods. "I'm okay." He smiles at her. "I guess I'm just preoccupied." He takes her hand and squeezes it.

She watches the passing stones. All these people were once alive. They were in love. They had dreams and families and homes. She shudders; cemeteries have always held a morbid fascination for her. Her aunt was a genealogist, and Christina remembers as a young girl the long hours spent with her in closed-up, dusty courthouse record rooms copying down dates and names; aching eternities crawling by as Aunt Ruth sat before microfilm readers and bent over crumbling census lists. But the cemeteries were different. Aunt Ruth showed her how to make rubbings off the tombstones by holding paper on the designs and scratching over it with a pencil, and this kept Christina busy while her aunt plodded across the grounds with a pen and a stenographer's pad. Most interesting of all were the ancient pioneer graveyards; in many of these there were no monuments as such, simply trees and rocks which served as markers. No names, no dates. Christina still wonders about these anonymous people and how their families knew to find the graves. Perhaps it was better that way, she thinks. Perhaps it was like cremation is now—scatter the ashes somewhere in the wind and set free the spirit instead of confining it to one place. But she knows the dead are not the ones confined; the living are.

At Ham's request, she sits in the car while he places the bouquet on Jill's grave. He kneels before the stone, motionless, and she wonders what he is doing. Praying? Crying? Talking to Jill?

She is surprised at the jolt of jealousy that strikes her, and immediately she is ashamed. Ham still mourns with a grief so intense it almost manifests itself physically. How can she be angry with him for that? How can she resent a man's loving his wife so much?

She watches him, his broad back bent in his navy suit, and she aches to touch him, to stroke the dark gray of his hair and press his flesh against hers. She wants to be on top of him, feeling him inside her, loving him. In any way she can, most of all, she wants to comfort him.

3

Kipp stands alone in the locker room, his bare feet cold on the concrete floor. He pulls on his practice clothes and sits down on the bench to lace up his shoes. He has not felt well all day, and he knows most of it is guilt. He saw the disappointment settle in his father's face last night when he told him he didn't want to go to the cemetery today. But hell! If Kipp has learned anything, he has come to understand that he is not responsible for his father's happiness. Only Ham can control that.

The locker room door bursts open and Coach Murphy thrusts his square-jawed face inside. "Bradford, you gonna stay in here all day?"

Kipp slams his locker. "On my way."

In the gym, half of the team is running laps on the floor while the rest work out in the weight room. Kipp starts down the steps toward the runners and the coach grasps his shoulder. "I want to see you in my office a minute."

"What for?"

"Just wanna talk to you."

Kipp follows Murphy into the coach's office. Murphy flips on the lights and roots through the small refrigerator. "Want some juice?"

"No thanks."

The coach grabs a small bottle of apple juice and falls back into his chair. "So how's life treating ya?"

"Fine."

Murphy twists off the cap and takes a sip of juice, glancing at a stack of papers on his desk. "I've been looking at your stats," he says. "You've really fallen off the past three, four weeks. I'm a little concerned." He tilts back in his seat, watching Kipp intently with his black eyes, stroking his chin. "Everything okay at home?"

Kipp shrugs. "Yeah."

"Classes going all right?"

"Yeah."

Murphy picks up a yellow inter-office memo. "Mr. Mills says you barely passed your algebra test."

Kipp blows out a breath and stares at the beaten wood of the coach's desk. He did not study at all for the test, so he was not surprised when he made a sixty on it. But the guilt he feels comes in knowing that he lied to his father about the grade; he doesn't give a shit about algebra. "I just had an off day," he says.

Coach Murphy takes another drink of juice. "I might believe that from anybody else," he says, "but up until this year you've had straight A's in math and science. You've been slipping the whole semester."

Rage begins to boil in Kipp's stomach. "So?"

"So I'm saying I think there's something wrong. Your performance on the court and in class is getting piss-poor. It's not up to what you used to do."

"There's nothing wrong." Kipp is trying hard to keep the anger out of his voice.

Murphy looks at him. "You doing any drugs?"

"No."

"Weed?"

"No."

"Using steroids?"

"No."

"You drink, Kipp?"

"Not too much."

Murphy leans back in his chair. "Why don't you lay off the booze for a while. I want you back up to where you used to be."

Kipp watches his shoes. "Can I go now?"

Murphy sighs. "Yeah. Go run some laps."

Kipp bolts for the door and sprints down the steps

to the gym floor, falling into place with the other runners. He didn't stretch, and now he'll probably get a muscle cramp.

Brett Mitchell is suddenly alongside him, his short brown hair clinging to the sweat on his forehead. "What'd the coach want?" he asks.

"Nothing," Kipp says. "He's a fucking idiot."

* * *

It is almost seven o'clock. Kipp and Brett are sitting in Brett's Camaro, which is parked on the shoulder of the dirt lane that leads to the county landfill. This spot is known as "the Road;" it is where they come often to do what they are doing now.

Kipp has Brett's biology book on his lap. Between his knees is a Zip-Loc bag of weed, and he is using the surface of the book to roll a joint. He licks the paper closed and twists the ends, then passes it to Brett. "Bon appétit," he grins.

Brett lights the joint and the sweet aroma fills the car. He slides a CD into the player and settles back in his seat as Led Zeppelin thunders from the speakers. "I love this old shit," he says.

Kipp finishes a second joint and lights it, pulling the smoke deep into his lungs. "Murphy asked me if I was doing drugs."

Brett glances at him. "No shit?"

"Can you believe that?"

"Hell, Jeff Saunders is so pumped up on steroids he's probably bullet-proof."

"And you can't tell me Murphy doesn't know it, either."

"Damn right he knows it. He's the one giving 'em to him I hear."

Kipp takes another drag off the joint. "He asked me if I was doing steroids."

Brett laughs. "Shoulda said, 'No, but I hear you got some you can give me.' Just to see his face."

"Right."

Brett blows out a long stream of smoke. It seems to cling to the cold windshield like ectoplasm. "How're things with you and Amber?"

"Fine."

"You don't ever say much about her."

"Nothing really to tell."

"You guys aren't broke up again are you?"

"No."

Brett sucks on the joint. "You're a lucky son-of-a-bitch to be dating Amber Merideth. Probably get to do the old ham-slam every night."

Kipp looks at him. "What's that supposed to mean?"

Brett gives him a wry glance. "C'mon, Bradford. Everybody knows Amber. She used to date Kenny Fisher, for chrissakes, and Kenny wouldn't go out with anybody if he couldn't get something."

Kipp grabs the front of Brett's shirt, and Brett's eyes widen in surprise. "Listen, asshole," Kipp tells him, "are you saying Amber's a whore?"

"No," Brett whines, pulling out of Kipp's grasp. "Take it easy, man. Jesus!" He shifts in his seat, distancing himself a little from Kipp. "You sure are uptight lately."

"Fuck you, Brett."

"What's wrong with you? I didn't mean anything by what I said."

Kipp stares out the window, not looking at him.

"Don't ever say anything like that again."

"Don't freak on me, man," Brett says, starting the engine. He pulls the car around and heads back toward the highway, spinning the wheels in the loose gravel, the joint sprouting from between his lips. "Jesus H. Christ."

4

Bruce has just clocked out. He pulls out of his smock and hangs it in his locker, then reaches for his coat. His eyes are bleary and tired, and he rubs his neck where a vague pain has begun to shoot up into his head.

Kelly, the morning shift clerk, steps into the cloak room. "Don't forget this," she says, holding up the bank bag with Bruce's store deposit in it.

"Thanks," he says, taking it from her.

She is tall and slim with long dark red hair that curls about her shoulders. Bruce has been interested in her since she came to work for the Gas-N-Pack a few months ago. He is fascinated with her eyes; they are large and brown, like a doe's eyes, he thinks. She is divorced and has a three-year-old daughter named Amanda and she smokes Salem 100s. That is all he knows about her.

She knows he has served time in prison, although he is fairly sure she doesn't know why. He can feel her growing attraction to him, though, and it both thrills him and frightens him. He knows as soon as she discovers he was accused of rape that her feelings for him will suddenly freeze. He has never been able to stay with one woman very long before she found out about him, and the relationships have always ended quickly and cleanly like an amputation. And that is one reason he is afraid to entangle his emotions with Kelly, because he likes her and is not eager to experience the pain of another loss.

He smiles at her as he passes. "Have a good day."

"You, too."

Outside in the brisk air, he shivers as he heads toward his 1992 Nissan. It is the only car he has ever owned, and even though he is ashamed of its peeling silver paint and ripped seats, it's paid for and the engine is good.

After dropping his bag in the bank's night depository, he winds his way through town toward home. Blake Shelton is on the radio, and for the first time in weeks, Bruce finds himself singing along. There is no doubt that Kelly's attraction to him is good for him; he suddenly feels confident, energized. He knows, of course, that ultimately the situation is doomed, and perhaps that is why he feels suddenly contented. Since Pamela, Bruce has not slept with a woman; that was over fifteen years ago, and the reality of sex, of sharing his body with someone terrifies him. But the idea, the thought, the fantasy, sustains him, and he discovers while talking to Kelly that half-asleep buzz of sexual pleasure that bubbles just below his conversations with her.

Bruce lives in Northside Mobile Home Park, a squalid collection of aging trailers that perch on a muddy hill overlooking the factories where most of his neighbors work. His is the first home on the loop, next door to the office. It is also one of the oldest, manufactured in the seventies with a rustic look— aluminum shutters and trim painted a sickly brown and yellow to resemble wood.

He has just stuck his key in the door when he notices the cat. It is large and black with one white ear, and it stares at him from the shelter it has found behind the garbage cans. Bruce has been seeing the cat for several days now; the first time it was hiding under his porch, its eyes two buttons of gold in the darkness. "Here, kitty," he says, starting toward it. The cat sits motionless for a moment, then darts away out of sight around the corner of the trailer.

Inside, Bruce finds two small bowls and fills one with tap water, then roots through his kitchen cabinets until he finds a can of tuna, which he opens and dumps in the other. "Here, kitty-kitty," he calls, stepping out onto the porch. The cat is still gone. He sets the bowls down and glances around one more time before going back inside.

Bruce slips off his shoes and pads toward the back of the trailer through the maze of papers, boxes, and strewn clothes, pulling out of his shirt as he enters the bedroom. God, he hates his body. He began to put on weight not long after he entered prison, and now it seems as though his belly just continues to grow, like some uncontrollable cancer. Even his tits are big, almost like a woman's, the nipples overly-large and pink.

He wishes his body looked like Gary's. Gary Hunter manages the trailer park. He and Bruce have become good friends over the years, living next door to each other. Sometimes they go out to clubs or movies; sometimes they get together to play cards or watch TV. During the summer Gary often works around the park without a shirt, and his lean body is burned brown by the sun. Bruce often watches Gary work, peeking ashamedly through the curtains, admiring his body; sometimes he masturbates while looking at Gary, although he always feels guilty afterwards. Still, he wonders how Gary would look naked, and he often fantasizes about Gary's penis.

Bruce steps out of his jeans and realizes he has an erection. He has never understood the overwhelming guilt that tortures him when he thinks about Gary, just as he has never understood the depression and anger he feels at himself for not being able to control his gay fantasies.

Although he had fooled around with his buddies during junior high school, he thought he'd outgrown all that by the time he got to high school, when he started dating girls. It was during his incarceration that Bruce had sex with a man for the first time. He was scared as hell, but he let the guy do him and he bled all night. During his seven years Bruce had relationships with about twenty different men. Some of them violently claimed others as "bitches," and Bruce was determined that would not happen to him. His strategy had been to bond with the larger guys, ones that could hold their own and protect him from assaults. It worked, and some of those men became more lovers than protectors.

Now Bruce feels confused. Sometimes he wonders if he is bisexual; sometimes he thinks he is just crazy, fucked-up. More than once after fantasizing about Gary, Bruce has been so overwhelmed with frustration, depression and chaos that he has wept. Crying makes him angry; anger makes him frustrated; frustration makes him depressed. There is no end to it.

Naked, he steps back into the living room and peeks out at the porch. The cat has been back and has eaten all the tuna. Bruce glances around the yard but doesn't see it. Maybe he will bring home some cat food tomorrow; maybe the cat will begin to trust him. He might even get it to come inside.

Bruce stares at the empty bowl and smiles.

THREE

1

Ham sits slumped in his chair, eyeing the pile of loan folders on his desk. There are at least twelve files, each needing some kind of documentation and each requiring him to make a personal phone call to tell someone the bank won't lend them the money they have asked for. Bullshit.

He drags the first one toward him and opens it. Leland Grant. Wants five hundred dollars to buy Christmas presents. No income but unemployment compensation, and not enough to cover his present obligations. Credit denied. Ham punches the number into the phone, feeling his stomach knot up as the call goes through.

"Hello?"

"Mr. Grant?"

"Yeah."

"Mr. Grant, this is Hamilton Bradford down at First State Bank. I'm calling you about your loan application."

"Yeah. When can I get my money?"

Ham scratches between his eyebrows with his thumbnail. "Well, that's why I'm calling. We reviewed your application, and I'm just afraid with your rent and your other bills that your income is just about stretched to its limit."

"So I don't get the money."

"I'm sorry. Even though we're only talking about a fifty-dollar-a-month payment, I don't think you can handle that right now."

"This is bullshit. I figured it up. After my bills I got almost two hundred dollars a month left over."

Ham looks back at the application. "You show you've got two dependents."

"That's right. My kids. I need the money for their Christmas."

"But you're talking about feeding and clothing two kids and yourself on a hundred and fifty dollars a month."

"I can do it. And if I get a job I can—"

"I just don't think so."

"This is bullshit, man."

A dull throb has begun behind Ham's eyes. "Mr. Grant, I'm trying to help you keep yourself out of a bind."

"Fuck you. You tell that to my kids on Christmas morning."

"Mr. Grant—" But he is gone. Ham hangs up the phone and stares at it, his stomach burning. "Shit."

Kay, his secretary, knocks on the door and sticks her head in. Her short blonde hair curls about her face, reminding him of Jill, and Ham supposes that's the reason he hired Kay three years ago. "Mr. Ham?"

"Yes, Miss Kay."

"Christina's on line two," she announces, smiling. She starts to withdraw, then looks at him again, concern on her face. "You okay?"

Ham manages a faint smile. "Fine."

"You look awful," she says, then closes the door.

He picks up the phone. "Hey, babe."

"Hi. How you doing?"

He gives a dry chuckle. "Well, I just got a vote of confidence from Kay; she told me I look awful. Oh, and I just got cussed out on the phone by a customer. Guess I'm doing fine."

Christina laughs. "Well, I won't keep you. I just called to find out what you want to do about dinner. Kipp's game starts at six-thirty."

Ham glances at his watch. It's going on five. "Why don't we just grab a burger or something on the way?"

"Sounds good to me. Is your dad going?"

"He talked like this morning he would."

"Good. Why don't you just pick me up here at the office? That would save us some time."

"Okay. Let me tie up some loose ends here and I'll be on over."

"All right. Love you, honey."

He puts the phone down and looks again at the loan folders. The rest can wait until tomorrow.

* * *

Ham helps his father ease down the front steps to the car waiting at the curb. Through the front passenger window, he can see Christina's mouth open in shock at Hamilton Senior's appearance; she has not seen him in several weeks, and Ham knows his dad has really deteriorated since then. "You sure you feel like going,

Dad?"

Hamilton Senior nods, smiling, not taking his gaze off the sidewalk. "Yeah. I wanna see Kipp play ball." Ham opens the door, and his father seems to melt into the back seat.

"Hi, Dad," Christina says.

He pats her shoulder. "Hi, honey."

"Glad you could come tonight."

"Me, too."

"You in?" Ham asks.

His dad nods. "I reckon."

Ham shuts the door and heads around the car. His hands are shaking. "Who's hungry?" he says, sliding in behind the wheel.

* * *

The air conditioning is turned off already for the winter, and the gymnasium is stuffy and humid like a summer day about to erupt in a thunderstorm. The pep band is blaring, and the trumpets careen wildly off key. Ham winces as the three of them pass the band on the way to their seats. His eyes search through the smoky crowd for Kipp; he spots a group of players milling about the locker room door, but Kipp is not among them.

Ham grasps his father's hand as he helps him slide onto the wooden bleachers. He had forgotten how hard the seats were. "Dad, you think you'll be able to sit all right on the bleachers?"

Hamilton Senior gives a nod, craning to see the gym floor. "Yeah. If I start getting stiff, I'll just get up and walk a little."

Ham looks at Christina. "Can you see okay, honey?"

"Fine." She is watching the crowd. Suddenly she waves. "There's Sandy!" she cries. Sandy Morris is Christina's partner in the real estate office and Christina's best friend. "I'll just go say hi." She slips out and darts up the steps. Ham watches her go, a tiny spark of jealousy in his chest.

He is just starting to contemplate this when the starting players are announced. He is not surprised to see Kipp sitting on the bench, elbows on knees and head resting on hands. Poor kid.

"The Star-Spangled Banner" is played by a brass quartet, and the crowd erupts in cheers as the song ends and the game begins.

Ham watches through the first two quarters as Kipp never moves from his seat. Oak Heights leads their opponent by four points at half-time, and the audience gives them an enthusiastic ovation as the teams head for the dressing rooms.

Christina is waving at Kipp, calling his name. "Over here!" she calls. He finally spots her and lifts his hand, his expression never changing. "What's wrong with him?" she says.

Hamilton Senior nudges his son. "Ham, can you help me to the restroom?"

"Sure, Dad." Ham takes his father's arm, leading him up the concrete steps toward the men's room. Inside, he stands behind Hamilton Senior at a urinal as the old man unzips his trousers and promptly pisses down the front of them, splashing his suede loafers and the tile floor. "Oh. . ." Hamilton Senior gasps.

Ham reaches over and pulls a handful of brown paper towels from the dispenser and begins swabbing at his father's khaki chinos. "Let me help," he says. A rotund, black-bearded man at the next urinal is watching them. Ham looks up at him. "Got a problem?"

The man looks quickly away, zips his jeans, and hurriedly flushes the urinal.

Hamilton Senior brushes at the dark wet spots across his thighs. "I can't go out of here like this."

"Why don't you let me walk in front of you?" Ham says. "And you can put your jacket over your lap when we sit down."

"I don't know what happened," his father is saying. "Sometimes I just can't make it in time." He laughs, but his voice is tinged with embarrassment and fear.

* * *

Kipp finally takes to the court during the fourth quarter when his team is twenty points ahead. He plays with no enthusiasm at all. Christina is shouting, "All right, Kipp! Defense!" Kipp turns and glares at her, sweat streaming down his face.

At that moment, one of the players passes the ball to Kipp. Kipp is just turning back to the game when the ball comes at him, knocking him squarely in the chest. The Oak Heights crowd begins to boo as Kipp falls to his hands and knees, gasping for breath.

Another player extends his hand to Kipp, but Kipp waves him away, climbing back up to his feet. The audience applauds. Kipp's face is flushed and angry as he heads off the court, clutching his stomach.

2

"I'm glad Kipp was all right," Christina says on the way home. "I wouldn't have yelled at him if I'd've known it would distract him."

"Don't worry about it," Ham says.

Christina watches the passing signs, not seeing them. She still feels guilty, somehow responsible for what happened. Above all, she can't put out of her head the expression in Kipp's eyes—the *anger*. He has never looked at her that way before.

"He never should've taken his eyes off the ball," Ham says. His voice is strangely flat and distant, his eyes never shifting from the road.

As Ham pulls the car into his father's drive, Hamilton Senior unbuckles his seatbelt. "Thanks for inviting me," he says. "Had a real good time."

Christina turns to look at him. "I'm glad you felt like going."

"Me, too," he says as Ham opens the door and helps him step out.

"G'night, Dad," she says, but the door has already slammed closed, and he doesn't hear her. She watches as Ham and his father shuffle toward the front door, the old man taking baby steps, his urine-stained trousers ballooning about his legs. He is talking to Ham; Christina can't hear them above the hum of the Escalade's engine, but she watches the action as if it were an old silent movie. Ham's hands seem so large against his father's back, and Christina shivers at how fast Hamilton Senior is going down.

When his father is safely in the house, Ham slides back into the driver's seat. "Ready?"

Christina nods, watching the house as the bathroom light comes on. "He had a good time," she says.

Ham nods. "Don't guess he's been to a game in twenty years. Not since Bruce was in school."

Christina pretends not to hear. She has only asked

about Bruce a couple of times, and her questions were met with cold, hard responses. She knows Ham is ashamed of his brother — not only because of what Bruce did, but because his conviction tarnished the family name. And she has learned to not bring up the subject or pursue it further.

"How old were you when your parents were killed?" Ham asks suddenly.

She looks at him, and in the light from the passing cars, she can see tears glistening in the corners of his eyes. She quickly glances away. "Thirty," she says. Her mother and father collided head-on with a drunk driver while they were returning from a friend's birthday party; all had died instantly. More than anything, Christina remembers the unreality of it all — how numb she felt as she stood before her parents' coffins and tried to understand the senselessness of it.

Ham watches the road, not wiping his eyes; tears brim over and spill down his cheeks. "Dad's dying," he says. "He's going to pieces right in front of me and I can't do a goddamned thing to stop it."

She reaches for his hand. "When do you take him to the doctor?"

"Tomorrow."

"Maybe it's not as bad as you think. Maybe the doctor can prescribe something—"

"Oh, hell, Chris!" he explodes. "You saw him tonight. You saw how he looks. He can barely walk, for crying out loud. He can't make it to the bathroom without pissing all over himself."

Christina's neck prickles, both in anger and fear. "Don't yell at me, Ham."

He wipes his eyes. "I'm sorry." He squeezes her

hand and glances at her. "I'm sorry, babe."

3

Kipp has showered and now stands in front of his open locker, buttoning his jeans. He still cannot believe he missed that pass. So fucking stupid. But Christina just wouldn't shut up. Her voice kept screeching out over everyone else until it was all he could hear.

Brett comes up behind him, slapping his shoulder. He is shirtless; he has started sprouting chest hair, and now he enjoys strutting around, showing it off. The prick. "Wanna go for a ride?" he asks.

"Nah." Kipp sits down on the bench to tie his sneakers. "Amber and I are going out."

"Oh, of course," Brett mutters, and Kipp glares at him. Brett grins and reaches down to pinch one of Kipp's nipples through his shirt. "Give her a squeeze for me, okay bro'?"

Kipp flies off the bench, grabbing Brett's neck and slamming his head into the row of lockers. The other guys are suddenly silent, watching. "Look, asshole," Kipp spits, "I'm damn sick and tired of your bullshit."

Brett's eyes are wide. "Shit, man, let go." His hands grab Kipp's arms, trying vainly to loosen the grip Kipp has on his neck. "Let go, man, I can't breathe!"

"Murphy!" someone barks. "Murphy's coming!"

Kipp lets Brett go with one last violent shove. Sweat has dripped onto Kipp's glasses and run down one lens, turning his vision into a smear. He stares into Brett's eyes, his rage too strong to put into words.

Murphy bounds into the room, glancing around at the other players and his gaze lights on Kipp and Brett in the corner. "What's going on in here?"

Kipp continues to stare at Brett. "Nothing," he says.

* * *

Kipp and Amber are parked on a dirt lane that leads to an abandoned strip pit. Nine Inch Nails is blaring from the CD player. Amber's mouth is hot as Kipp explores it with his tongue. His erection strains against his jeans, throbbing with the beat of the music. Amber's nipples stiffen beneath his fingertips. She moans, and Kipp buries his face in the curls of her red hair, moving his other hand toward his crotch. His fingers pinch her nipples, and she jerks away.

"Not so hard," she whispers. She kisses him again, stroking his back and shoulders.

Kipp can stand it no longer. His fingers fumble with his fly, setting his erection free. It stands stiff and throbbing. "Suck it," he whispers.

Amber pulls away and looks at him. "Wh—what?"

"Suck it," he says again. "Do it."

She slides away from him, buttoning her blouse. "No."

He feels his cheeks flush. "Why not?"

"I don't want to." She sits back in her seat, turning toward the window. "I think you oughta take me home.

"What's wrong with you?" he asks.

"Just take me home."

"Not 'til you tell me what's wrong with you." He realizes his erection has wilted, and he covers himself with his hands, hurrying to close his fly. He glances at her face, grateful that the dark hides her eyes. "What's wrong?" he asks again.

"Something's the matter with you," she croaks, and he realizes she is on the verge of tears. "It. . . it's not the same anymore. You never used to be like this. So rough." Her hand covers her face and he knows that now she *is* crying. "'Suck it,'" she says, imitating him. "How do you think that makes me feel?"

Kipp stares toward the ceiling. "I'm sorry," he mutters. "I thought. . . I don't know. I thought you'd want to."

"Well, I don't. It's like just coming up to me and saying, 'Fuck me,' and expecting me to plop down and spread my legs," she says, her voice cracking. "It makes me feel like a whore."

Kipp thinks about Brett, about how the prick had intimated that Amber *was* a whore, and fresh rage flows through him. "I said I was sorry. What more do you want me to do?"

"You sound real concerned." Her cell phone rings and she moves to dig it out of her purse, wiping her eyes with the back of her hand. She looks at the screen. "Shit, it's my mom." She punches "Ignore."

Kipp starts the engine and pulls the car around, heading back toward the highway. He turns down the music; it's starting to rub his nerves raw. "I'll take you home."

She reaches for his hand, but he jerks it away. "I'm sorry, Kipp," she whispers. "But something's wrong with you. You're different." When he doesn't answer her, she looks out the window, toward the outside, toward the dark.

4

Bruce comes awake slowly as the mid-afternoon sun leaks into his bedroom from around the window shades. He covers his eyes with his arm, but he is awake now, and he knows it will be impossible to get back to sleep. Impossible because now he is thinking about her again, about Kelly.

She smiled at him—*really* smiled—this morning when she breezed in and he told her she looked pretty. There was a light in her eyes he had never seen before, and he wonders now if maybe that light was for some other guy, maybe a guy she woke up beside who kissed her chestnut hair and told her he loved her. But she smiled at *him* nonetheless.

He wonders how it would be to wake up beside her, to watch her body stretch in the early light, to feel her bare skin against his own. But that is just a fantasy. Sometimes he wonders if he will ever make love again with anyone, and sometimes he thinks that just being with someone—without the sex—might be enough. And even though the thought of never again experiencing the magic of sex depresses him, it is not wholly terrifying to him as it once was.

Perhaps he should go ahead and ask Kelly out. Maybe the fact that he was falsely convicted of rape wouldn't matter to her, especially since he has never given her any reason to fear him.

His eyes open wide. *No!* He is doing it again. He is letting his fear of being alone take control. Whenever he gets this way, whenever his loneliness surfaces, he always does something stupid. He will *not* get into another dead-end relationship. No matter how he might try to reason with himself, tell himself she won't care and that it won't matter, he knows that in the end she *will* care. It *will* matter. Once she finds out he was accused of rape, her whole perception of him will cloud over, and his every action will be a threat to her.

No, it's best to just leave it alone, to let the fantasy play out. It's the surest way to not get hurt again.

He sits up in bed, swiping a hand through his oily hair. The sheet falls to his waist, exposing his round belly. He was a fool to even think a fantasy like that could come true.

* * *

The afternoon is hot and dry, especially for November. All the weathermen are talking about it. Bruce pulls on a pair of black shorts and a Michigan State T-shirt and steps outside.

He has not seen the cat in a couple of days, although he finally bought a sack of cat food and he leaves a bowl of it and water out every day. Some animal is eating it, but he isn't sure if it's his cat or not.

He smiles to himself. *His* cat. Funny. He should ask Gary if he knows anything about it.

At the other end of the trailer park, he sees three black guys on the fenced-off basketball court shooting hoops. He knows them only by their first names, and he knows they all live here at Northside. He ambles toward them. Sometimes the four of them will play a game, two on two.

Marcus is the first to spot him. "Hey, there's Bruce," he tells the others, grinning. Marcus is short and stocky with a shaved head and a whisper of a mustache. James and Andre turn to see him. James is tall—well over six feet —and bone-thin; he always wears a black tank and a black ball cap. Andre is light-skinned and pudgy like Bruce; he throws up a hand in greeting. "It's the Bruce Man," he cries.

"How you guys doing?" Bruce says, stepping through the gate and slapping James a high-five. It seems strange to Bruce that these three men are probably the only friends he has besides Gary, and that he knows so little about them. James and Andre are married and work at the plastics factory; Marcus is still in high school. That is the extent of Bruce's knowledge of them.

"How about a game?" James asks him.

"Sure."

Marcus bounces the ball around them and sinks it through the rusty netless hoop. "Me and Bruce'll take on you guys," he says.

Bruce remembers the cat. "Any of you seen a black cat around here with one white ear?"

They look at him. James scratches his head. "Don't think so."

Bruce shrugs. "Been hanging around my trailer. Just wondered if it belonged to anybody."

Andre shakes his head. "Ain't seen it."

"Let's play," Marcus says.

* * *

Twenty minutes later, when Bruce and Marcus are six points ahead, Andre calls a time-out. "I need a rest," he says, plopping down on the pavement. He lies back, stretching out with his hands under his head.

Bruce chuckles, stepping to the edge of the court toward the street, wiping off his sweaty face with the tail of his shirt.

At that moment, a little red Escort putters by. The driver waves at him, and for a moment Bruce is stunned. Then he realizes it's Kelly. He stares after her as she disappears over the hill, his shirttail still in his hands. He has forgotten how to breathe.

FOUR

1

Ham and his father are sitting in Dr. Steinfield's waiting room with its Lysol smell and its dusty blinds open to the hot morning sun outside. Hamilton Senior is studying the patterns in the ancient tile floor. Ham pretends to read a three-month-old issue of *Time*, occasionally giving a side glance to his father. He has checked his phone three times for texts from Christina, but he's heard nothing from her all morning.

They have been waiting for only twenty minutes, but the pounding in Ham's chest makes it seem like an hour. He is not sure why he is so nervous. But his hands are shaking and beads of sweat have popped out on his forehead. Beside him, Hamilton Senior is strangely calm and relaxed. Across the room, the only other patient waiting is an elderly woman with purplish-gray hair and cat's-eye glasses; she smiles and nods at Ham.

Dr. Steinfield's nurse pokes her head out of the

back hall. "Mr. Bradford?"

Ham helps his father stand, and they shuffle toward the door. "Hi, Nancy," his father says, grinning at the nurse.

She holds the door open for them. "Hello, Mr. Bradford," she says, too loudly. "How we doing this morning?"

"All right."

She smiles faintly at Ham, and he gives her a nod; he turned her down for a loan last year, and she seems to not have forgiven him for it. She shows them into an examination room, and his father climbs onto the table, the paper rustling beneath him. Nancy slips a thermometer into Hamilton Senior's mouth and a blood pressure cuff on his arm. "Temperature's fine," she says, "blood pressure's a little high." She notes it on his chart. "Are you a little nervous today?"

Her voice is starting to grate on Ham's nerves. She is so damned *loud*, as if she is talking to a deaf child.

"No," his father answers. "I'm all right."

She nods and scribbles something. "He'll be here in a minute." And then she is gone.

His father looks at him. "Kipp okay this morning?"

Ham nods. "He seems fine. I don't guess that ball took much out of him."

They drift into uncomfortable silence. Ham watches his father sitting on the table, the old man's legs dangling above the floor. He seems so small and fragile, like a newborn.

Dr. Steinfield bursts through the door, his thinning black hair hanging in an unkempt comma on his forehead. He shakes Hamilton Senior's hand. "Mr. Bradford." He nods at Ham. "Doing okay?"

"Fine." Ham has never cared much for Steinfield. He is originally from New Jersey and his haughty personality has not transferred well to the South.

The doctor is looking into Hamilton Senior's eyes with a penlight. "Say you've been dizzy?"

"A little. More weak than anything."

"Any aches and pains?"

"In my back and sides." He points vaguely to his hips. "Down low."

Ham clears his throat. "He's having some trouble getting to the bathroom in time."

Steinfield looks at him, then back at Hamilton Senior. "That right?"

Ham's father nods. "Sometimes I just don't make it."

"You having to go more than usual?"

"Seems like it. Especially in the night."

Steinfield is writing on the chart. "Any pain or discomfort when you urinate?"

"Not really."

"Trouble getting the stream started?"

Hamilton Senior looks up. "Yeah. Now that you mention it. If I get to the bathroom in time, sometimes I feel like I have to stand there a while before I can go."

The doctor sets the chart down. "I guess the next thing we need to do then is a digital prostate exam." He reaches for a package of latex gloves. "Drop your trousers and lean over the table, please."

Ham helps his father off the table and unbuckles the old man's pants and lets them fall to the floor. He tugs his father's dingy briefs down his legs. "Okay,

Dad, bend over."

Steinfield lubricates his finger and steps behind Hamilton Senior. Ham looks away as his father winces.

"You still play golf, Ham?" the doctor asks.

"Sometimes," Ham answers, looking at the floor. "Don't seem to have as much time as I used to."

"I know how that is," the doctor answers, and Ham wonders how he can carry on such a conversation with his finger stuck up another man's ass. "I haven't been out to the course since September myself." He looks at the ceiling a moment, his jaw working, and Ham realizes for the first time that the doctor is chewing gum. "How's it feel when I press on that?" he asks Hamilton Senior.

Ham's father grunts. "Hurts."

Steinfield nods. "Your prostate's enlarged a bit since the last time I checked it. That's not unusual." He withdraws his hand and peels the glove off, handing Hamilton Senior a box of tissues to wipe himself with. "But you're having quite a bit of pain and some other symptoms, and I think we ought to do some tests."

"What kind of tests?" Ham says.

The doctor looks at him. "Specifically? A biopsy. I felt several nodules on his prostate, and I think we need to get those checked out pronto." He writes something on his chart. "I'll get Nancy to make you an appointment at the hospital."

Ham looks at him. "So we're talking something pretty serious here."

Steinfield is still writing. "Maybe." He tears off a paper and gives it to Ham. "Maybe not. That's why we need to get it checked out. Just to be sure."

Ham looks at the paper in his hand. It is a

prescription. "Get that filled for him," Steinfield tells him. "It'll help with the pain and discomfort."

Ham watches his father struggle with pulling up his underwear, and his numbness gives way to fear.

2

The office has been super busy all morning. Christina leans back in her chair and stares out at the street. The sun is bright and hot, and the weathermen all seem to be astounded at the warmth of this month.

Ham just called, telling her about Dad's visit to Dr. Steinfield. His voice was shaky, and she wonders now if he had been crying. She thinks of him sitting in his office, looking at those dark paneled walls and those horrible modern art prints the bank insists on plastering up down there. God, that room is enough to depress anybody.

Sandy knocks lightly on the doorframe. Her round eyes are concerned. "You okay, Chris?"

Christina nods. "Ham just called. His dad has to go in for some tests next week. He's pretty upset."

Sandy sets a cup of coffee on Christina's desk. "I thought you looked like you could use this."

Christina gives her a grateful smile. "Thanks. I haven't had a chance to get any since my first cup." She takes a sip. Too much sugar, but she will drink it anyway.

Sandy slides into the chair across from the desk. "What kind of tests?"

"Prostate biopsy."

Sandy nods. "My dad had that done."

Christina watches the window. "I'm really worried about Ham," she says. "He's so depressed. He was crying last night."

Sandy blows on her coffee. "Why don't you take him out for dinner or something? Do something that will cheer him up."

Christina shakes her head. "I don't know. This is different from just having a case of the blues. He's been like this for quite a while."

"How long?"

"Ever since. . . " *Since Jill died*, she thinks. "A while."

"That sounds serious, Chris. Maybe he should see a doctor."

Christina shrugs. "Maybe. The only way I'd probably get him to go is if I made him think it was his decision. I don't think he'd take kindly to that kind of suggestion."

Christina has known Sandy since high school, since they were giggly girls who used to hold slumber parties in Sandy's basement. Christina remembers all those times of staying up late, setting up Sandy's record player and dancing to the Bee Gees and Shaun Cassidy, and of sneaking cigarettes under the basement stairs. And then there were the times when Christina was married to Kevin, when she would manage to escape for a few hours and hide out at Sandy's apartment, crying until her eyes were drained of tears, listening to Sandy try to console and counsel. And even after Sandy had married and her two sons had been born, Christina was still able to trust her. And looking back, Christina realizes that Sandy has never given her any bad advice; after all, it was Sandy who suggested that Christina return to school for her degree.

She takes a drink of the too-sweet coffee. "Maybe

I'll mention it to him," she says.

3

It is mid-afternoon. School was over forty-five minutes ago.

Kipp sits in a desk in the front row, watching as Mr. Mills paces back and forth in front of him, lecturing him about his algebra grades. What a cocksucker, Kipp thinks. He glances at his watch. Three-thirty. He is supposed to be at basketball practice right now, but apparently it was Coach Murphy who arranged this little meeting.

This day has been nothing but shit. He saw Amber once between second and third periods, when she said she was having lunch with one of her friends. No explanation, but he knows it was because of last night. Brett didn't say much all day, but Kipp really doesn't care whether or not the prick talks to him. And then, at the end of sixth period, Mills nailed him to stay after for a "little chat." What a fucking moron.

He is failing algebra. That much he already knows. Not that he really gives a shit.

"Why do you think you're failing my class?" Mills asks him, bending down into his face.

Kipp looks at him, then at the blackboard behind. "I don't know."

"Do you study for this class?"

"Not much."

Mills blows out a breath and walks back to his desk. "Then I can't help you much." He stacks a pile of papers. "It's up to you to pass or fail this course. You can't expect to make the grade if you don't put much into it."

"I know."

Mills sits down in his chair. "Do you like this class?"

Kipp looks at the ceiling. "Not really."

"Is there anything I might could do or change to make you like it better?"

Kipp blows out a breath. When is this idiot ever going to shut up? "Probably not." It won't do any good to tell Mills that he doesn't understand a damn thing about algebra. The whole concept is a bunch of shit. It's like a silly game—$2x - 4y = 3x + 1y$. What the hell kind of mathematics is that? And who gives a flying fuck? And who can possibly use this bullshit in everyday life?

Mills looks at him. "You know, Coach Murphy tells me that if you fail this semester of algebra, you're off the team." He scratches at his closely-cropped blond hair; he wears it in a flat-top, and Kipp supposes he does that to make himself look "cool." God, he loathes this man. "Are you aware that your position on the basketball team is in danger if you don't get your grades up?"

"Yeah."

Now Mills stares at the ceiling. "You know, Kipp, this is the first class of mine you've ever been in, but from what I understand from some other teachers, you're a brilliant young man. Straight A's until this semester."

Oh, shit, here it comes, Kipp thinks.

Mills looks at him. "Something is definitely wrong. But Coach Murphy, me—all of your teachers—we're all concerned about you." He clears his throat. "One teacher said she's noticed that you tend to stay by yourself more this year."

Rage is boiling in Kipp's gut. "Is that all you all do in teachers' meetings?" he explodes. "Sit around and talk about me?"

Mills holds up his hands. "Calm down, Kipp." He sighs. "No, that's not all we do. But from time to time we do bring up a student in conversation that we're particularly worried about. Like you."

"Don't worry about me," Kipp says.

Mills looks at him hard, then heads to open the door to the hallway. "Kipp, I don't know what's wrong with you, and it's obvious you're not going to tell me. But please, *please*, man, talk to somebody about it. Go to the school counselor—that's what she's there for. Talk to your dad. Talk to a minister. Just try to get yourself straightened out before you do something stupid."

Kipp blows out a breath. "Can I go now?"

Mills nods, looking at the floor. "Yeah, you can go. Just think about what I've said."

Kipp heads out into the hall, brushing past Mills and biting the inside of his jaw to keep from telling the son-of-a-bitch off. He'll go straight home and skip practice today; Coach Murphy can go fuck himself.

4

Bruce is sitting on his front porch, his feet dangling just above the brown, late-autumn grass, the sun hot on his face. The cat is peeking at him from behind the garbage can, its eyes round, its tail twitching. "Here, kitty," Bruce whispers.

He has been sitting here for ten minutes. Beside him is a bowl of fresh food, and he hopes that hunger will eventually win out and the cat will venture toward the smell. Then maybe he can touch it. But the cat seems determined to crouch in safety while Bruce is there.

Kelly seemed pleased this morning when Bruce commented about her driving by yesterday. She told him her mother lives in the area and she had been up for a visit. And she was happy to find out Bruce lived in the trailer park; she asked him about his home and how he liked it there. He lied and said he loved it, that his trailer was "nice and cozy." God. *Cozy*. What an idiot he was. And then later when he spotted himself in the rear-view mirror of his car, he saw he had a smear of peanut butter on his chin.

"Here, kitty," he calls again. The cat has stuck its head out into the sunlight, its nose wet and twitching, sniffing the aroma of food on the air. "C'mon," Bruce says. He sits stone-like as the cat inches its way toward him, and Bruce nearly cries out when the cat leaps onto the porch to sniff at the bowl. It eyes him suspiciously, then bends over the food.

"Good kitty," Bruce whispers. Slowly, he begins moving his hand toward the cat's head, until his trembling fingers hover just above the dusty black fur. He touches the cat's head, and it sits up, glaring at him, then crouches back over the bowl. Bruce strokes it again, and the cat merely looks at him without moving away. The third time Bruce pets it, the cat begins to purr, faintly at first, then louder.

Suddenly, there is a shuffling sound behind them. Bruce turns to see Gary ambling up the drive. He is shirtless and wearing a pair of cargo shorts. The cat darts away, toward the back of the trailer out of sight.

"Whatcha doing, Bruce?"

"Feeding that cat," Bruce tells him, motioning toward the direction the animal fled. He eyes Gary's chiseled body, the fine hair that trails down his chest to his stomach and disappears into his shorts. Immediately, he looks away. "Yeah, I've been feeding it tuna, but I finally got some cat food."

Gary spits. "Goddamned strays."

Bruce ignores his tone. "You seen it before? Know if it belongs to anybody?"

Gary shakes his head. "Doesn't belong to anybody I know." He rubs at his bearded chin. "So what've you been doing with yourself? Ain't seen you around much lately."

"I've been here," Bruce says. "I just sleep and work. That's about it." He considers telling Gary about Kelly, but then he doesn't. He's afraid of talking about it, as if telling someone he is falling in love will cause it to end.

Gary pulls a pack of Winstons out of his back pocket and lights one up. "Well, I saw you outside and thought I'd come over see how you were doing. Wanna smoke?"

"Nah."

Gary takes a drag. "You have any nights off this week?"

"Tomorrow," Bruce tells him.

"Well, I wanted to go bar-hopping. You wanna go?"

Bruce shrugs. "Sure." He and Gary haven't done much together since the end of summer. Gary has been busy the past couple of months doing maintenance in preparation for winter. "Whatcha got in mind?"

Gary takes another draw off his cigarette. "There's this new club out on the boulevard, the All-Star or something like that. Supposed to have a bunch of big-screen TVs and shit." He blows out a stream of smoke. "Nothing else, we can go there and watch the Giants beat the shit out of Dallas."

Bruce nods. "Sounds good," he lies. He hates football. But the idea of actually getting out and going somewhere—even if it's not with Kelly—appeals to him, and he can feel excitement building in his chest.

Gary nods and heads back toward his trailer. "Come on over tomorrow night around seven."

Bruce watches Gary walk away, and he realizes he has an erection. He crosses his legs, hoping Gary didn't notice. God, he hates this! He does not want to feel sexual toward Gary. He does not want to be a faggot. What would Gary think if he knew?

But then maybe Gary *does* know. Maybe he has seen Bruce staring at him and masturbating frantically behind the threadbare curtains. Maybe Gary is trying to come on to him, to seduce him. Maybe Gary can sense Bruce's attraction, and he is aroused by it. Maybe Gary is just curious. Or maybe it is all in Bruce's head; Gary has never given any real indication that he is gay. He has always talked about women in a sexual way, and several times when he and Bruce have been out together at clubs, Gary has danced with the most attractive girls, holding them close and kissing them, sometimes disappearing outside with them for a time.

Bruce wonders how it would be to hold Gary, to feel his hard body pressing against his own, to feel Gary's muscles moving beneath his shirt. He wonders how it would be to live with Gary, to sleep beside him every night and feel him breathing and dreaming in the dark.

But what about Kelly? Wouldn't it feel just as good with her? Or better? And what would she think if she knew he was sitting here on his front porch fantasizing about another man?

He hates himself when he gets like this. His need for someone is so strong—and not just the need for sex. Most of all, he needs a partner, a companion. Someone to be with.

Tears have filled his eyes. Why is he like this? He is such a goddamned faggot. Why can't he just be a normal man with normal desires?

Across the yard, the cat sits in the shadow of the garbage can, crouching, watching.

FIVE

1

The Saturday sun is bright but cooler than it has been the past few days. Ham is standing on the golf course at Lakeview Country Club, staring at the third green and facing the cool breeze as it rushes over his face.

Beside him, Ray Nelson is concentrating on driving his ball toward the flag. "Damn wind," he mutters as he swings and the ball barely edges onto the green circle of grass. "I'd've birdied this hole if the wind had let up."

Behind them, Russ Mitchell sits on his golf cart, his round belly quivering as he suppresses his laughter. "Always got some kind of excuse, Ray," he says.

"Stick it up your ass," Ray tells him. He swipes the back of one hand across his black mustache and trudges up the hill toward the green.

Russ laughs again. "This is what I get for playing with a couple of old men." He shakes his head, and his short dark-red curls jiggle along with his stomach.

Ham smiles, tugging at his cap and trudging along behind Ray, using his iron as a cane. Russ is ten years younger than he and Ray, and he always looks for a chance to jab at their ages. "You'll get yours," Ham says, and Russ guffaws as he careens the cart up to the edge of the green.

Ham takes a deep breath. It feels good to be out here again, sweating a little and walking over the still-wet grass, listening to Ray curse and bitch and Russ annoy them with his insane cackling. He has played golf with them off and on now for about seven years. Ray, in spite of his terrible game, is a very competent doctor in family practice. Russ is a senior foreman in the plastics factory, and Ham imagines that he must have a fairly decent income to belong to the country club. Russ' son, Brett, and Kipp are good friends, and the four of them have gone a few times to Lexington to see the Wildcats play when Ham could get the tickets.

"Shit!" comes Ray's exasperated cry.

Russ slaps his ample thigh, hollering with laughter. "He missed! Goddamn, I can't believe it! He missed that putt!"

Ray scowls at Russ. "Shut the fuck up. I'll take you on in tennis any day."

Ham grins; he would like to see Russ pounding and huffing and sweating on a tennis court.

Russ tees off on the next hole and heads for the cart. "I'll go on and drive up to the green," he says. "See you girls in a minute."

"That bastard makes me so damn nervous," Ray

says as Russ sputters away. He takes his position beside the ball. "How's your dad doing?" he asks.

Ham shrugs. "Well as can be expected. He goes in for a prostate biopsy next week."

Ray looks up at him, then back to the ball. "Who's his doctor?"

"Steinfield."

Ray nods. "I know James. He's a good doctor. A little short on the bedside manner, but he knows what he's doing." He tees off, watching the ball fly toward the green, where Russ has just pulled up.

"Good shot," Ham says. He places his ball.

"How're *you* doing?" Ray asks. "You seem kinda down."

Ham blows out a breath and looks at him. "To be honest, I don't feel so good. I'm just. . . depressed."

Ray nods. "I'm sure you got a lot on your mind with your father and all."

"Yeah."

"Been depressed long?"

Ham nods. "Yeah. Seems like forever."

"Before your dad got sick?"

"Yeah."

Ray looks away across the course, toward the clubhouse with its Victorian turrets and gleaming spires. "Why don't you come in to see me next week? How long's it been since you had a good physical?"

Ham grunts. "A while. Several years."

"Call and make an appointment first thing Monday morning. Let's try to rule out anything physical that might be dragging you down."

Ham looks at him. "You think I might need a shrink?"

Ray shakes his head. "Won't know 'til I look at you."

Ham swings and the ball lands in the rough. He looks at Ray. What does he really think of him? Does he think he's crazy? The thought of going to a psychiatrist is scary; it's the loss of control, the idea that his mind may be caving in on itself.

Ray looks around, an incredulous look on his face. "Shit!" he shrieks. "Damn Russ took our clubs!"

2

Christina backs her car out of the garage and glances back at her small house. A cottage, that's what it is, really. A kitchen, living room, and bath downstairs and one bedroom upstairs. She remembers how excited she had been when she had first found it. Just the right size for one person. And she was so happy to finally be out of her parents' house and on her own again. She immediately began decorating—using the eclectic chic look before it was really popular. But she's seen very little of it the past few months, spending most of her time at Ham's.

Poor Ham. She thinks back on the conversation she had with Sandy yesterday, and she wonders again how she will bring up the subject of Ham's going to see a doctor about his depression. But he is not getting any better. Thursday night after the ball game was the worst she has seen him—crying and blabbering and cursing. Maybe it's all the stress with his dad. Maybe it's still Jill's death. Maybe it's his work. She doesn't know.

She understands his concern for his dad, though. That poor man is really sick. She knows she had an unmaskable expression of disgust on her face the other night when he returned from the restroom with urine all over his trousers and shoes. At the same time, though, she knows Dad was embarrassed and ashamed of himself, and that makes her feel even guiltier about her reaction.

But the man is going fast. That is clear. And she knows Ham is taking it hard.

Christina pulls into Ham's driveway behind Kipp's car. She is not surprised that Kipp is still here on a Saturday morning; some Saturdays he sleeps until after noon.

She opens the front door with her key and slips inside. Ham is playing golf this morning with Ray and Russ. She decided that today she would surprise him with a special lunch when he came home, so she has brought a bag of groceries with her—chicken breasts to broil with basil, pasta salad, and a bottle of white zinfandel.

She sets the bag down in the kitchen and starts to put the chicken and wine in the refrigerator when she hears something in the den. She moves to the door and peeks around through the dining room. Is Kipp awake?

The television is on—cartoons. She turns it down and glances around the room. Kipp must have been up. The worn quilt from his bed is splayed across the couch, and a half-eaten bowl of soggy Cheerios sits on the coffee table. "Kipp?" she calls. "Kipp?" He must have gone back to bed.

She moves down the hall. Now she can hear music blaring in Kipp's room—one of those metal bands he likes—and she supposes that's why he didn't hear her. "Kipp?"

And then she notices the smell—sweet and herbal, like something cooking. Kipp's door is open just a crack. She starts to knock and her hand hits the door. It swings open wide.

Kipp is lying on his bed in his underwear, his glasses off. He sits straight up as the door opens. "Jesus Christ!" he cries. "What the hell are you doing?"

Christina begins backing away. "Sorry, Kipp. I called—" And then her gaze falls on his hand, where the joint sits smoking between his fingers. She is so shocked that it takes a moment for her to realize that it is pot and not just a cigarette.

Kipp's face is red and pinched. "You always barge into people's rooms without knocking?"

Christina backs into the hall. "I'm sorry," she says again, closing the door. She leans against the wall and stares at the ceiling. "Oh, my God," she whispers.

3

Kipp stubs out the joint and grabs his glasses. Fuck. He crawls out of bed and pulls on a pair of gym shorts, running his hand through his hair; it feels greasy. He turns the stereo down and looks at his tousled sheets. His head hurts and he feels sleepy. He flops back onto the bed, staring at his poster of Kate Upton on the wall.

"Shit," he whispers. What is he going to do now? He knows Christina will probably tell his dad. And then Ham will come down hard on him. But fuck! How could the bitch just walk in on him like that without knocking? But at least he wasn't flogging his log or anything.

He reaches down to the floor and picks up his Zip-Loc bag of weed and sits swinging it between his knees. He wonders if Ham will search his room. As far as he knows, Ham has never rifled through his things, and Kipp has always just kept his stuff in his bedside drawer. But until now, Ham has never had any reason to look for anything in here, and Kipp supposes he should put his weed somewhere else.

He falls back onto the bed. But shit, it's not like he's a kid or anything. Hell, he's been smoking weed since he was thirteen. Brett introduced him to it once when Kipp was spending the night; that was the time they sneaked up into Brett's attic and smoked joints behind a wall of musty cardboard boxes. Brett has introduced him to all sorts of things, including beer.

Maybe he has been too hard on Brett the past couple of weeks. After all, Brett is his best friend, even if he is a prick. Even if he thinks Amber is a whore.

Kipp blows out a breath. Amber. Shit. He's not sure how he feels about her anymore. Last night he saw she had changed her Facebook relationship status to "It's Complicated." How could she just kiss him off like that? And over something so stupid. It wasn't as if he asked her to commit murder or anything. A lousy blowjob. That's all he wanted.

His phone buzzes and he grabs it off the bedside table. It's a text from Brett. *U up?*

Just got caught 420, Kipp responds.

No shit???? LMFAO Ur dad?

Christina.

He stares at the ceiling. His phone vibrates with another text from Brett, but he doesn't look at it. Sooner or later he'll have to go out of his room and face

Christina. Sooner or later he'll have to apologize for exploding at her.

Fuck.

4

A crisp evening wind cuts around Bruce's face as he locks his door. He glances around for the cat, but it's apparently huddled up someplace warm—under the trailer perhaps. He pulls the collar of his jacket up around his neck and heads toward the lights of Gary's place.

He has been nervous all afternoon. He's not sure why. Down deep he feels an anxious stirring, and the arousal seems to cut through the nervousness. He masturbated in the shower.

He still wonders what this means—Gary's asking him to go out tonight. (He winces at that; it almost sounds like he and Gary are going on a date, like two queens.) But perhaps it means nothing—that Gary simply wanted someone to go bar-hopping with.

Or maybe he wants to be with me, Bruce thinks. He stops two steps from Gary's front door, almost afraid to knock. Kelly floats through his mind—fragile and waif-like—and then she is gone and Bruce is rapping on the metal door.

Gary pokes his head out. His hair is wet and he is wearing only a towel. "You're early, man," he tells him.

* * *

Gary has a new Charger, dark blue with a charcoal interior. He turns up the Jason Aldean CD as they cruise down the boulevard. "You like country?" he asks.

Bruce nods. "Yeah. Not much rock I like anymore."

"I know what you mean. I hate that rap shit."

They pull into the crowded lot of the All-Star; its sign is ringed with baseballs, footballs, soccer balls, and basketballs. Bruce can already hear the thump of the music inside—can feel it in his chest. Inside, the walls are plastered with sports paraphernalia—a few autographed football jerseys, pennants, caps, and other junk. Various games are playing on all the televisions and an old Bruce Springsteen song is screaming out of the sound system. Gary points toward an empty booth, and they slide in behind the table.

A waitress appears immediately. She is black, petite, and her hair is pulled back into a short ponytail. Gary orders a pitcher of beer, then pulls off his jacket. "Cool place," he comments.

Bruce looks around. "Yeah."

"So how's things going?" Gary asks. "How's work?"

Bruce gives him a half-smile. "All right." Again he thinks of telling Gary about Kelly, but he doesn't. But this time he is not sure why. Maybe he secretly wants Gary to think he is gay.

Gary lights a cigarette, and they sit in silence until the waitress reappears with the beer. As she moves away, Bruce leans over the table. "She's cute," he says, nodding toward her.

Gary takes a drag off his cigarette and pours a glass of beer. "I ain't into black meat myself." He looks around. "Looks like everybody here's with somebody." He picks up his glass and takes a sip, leaving a trace of foam on his black mustache. Bruce looks at his fingers—long and sinewy, the nails strong and square, the knuckles covered with fine black hair.

What does Gary really think of him? Does he truly think of him as a good friend? Or does he merely see him as a possible fag, someone to get a simple sexual kick with? Or does he see him as a tormented queer to toy with and tease? But maybe he is reading too much into Gary. Gary probably doesn't even think about Bruce sexually at all. But Bruce looks at him, and he fantasizes about the body across from him under the tight t-shirt and Levi's, and he feels that longing in his gut again, thudding like a drum.

And he comes to two possibilities:

One: Gary wants to sleep with him, although he is not sure Bruce would be willing to, and he is unsure of how to approach him. Whether he is simply curious about having sex with a man or he has done this before, Bruce doesn't know. But this trip tonight may be one step closer. Gary may be testing the waters. Perhaps the scene tonight with the bath towel wrapped around his waist was a set-up, something to simply gauge Bruce's reaction. And if that's the case, Bruce knows the expression on his face must have been unquestionable.

Two: Bruce is imagining all this. Gary is completely straight and has no desire or intention to sleep with him. All of Gary's little tricks and ploys are nothing more than Bruce's demented fantasies—manifestations of his sexual confusion. Bruce is thinking too much, fantasizing too much. Maybe he needs to concentrate all that energy on Kelly.

But Kelly doesn't have a rock-hard chest and broad shoulders. Kelly doesn't have that line of hair trailing down her stomach.   And, most of all, Kelly doesn't have a penis.

* * *

When Gary finally pulls the Charger back into the trailer park it is almost two-thirty. He and Bruce are very drunk, and they have been singing loudly to a Luke Bryan song. "I'm glad you went, pal," Gary says thickly. "We need to do this again real soon." He pats Bruce's shoulder with a hint—just a hint—of a squeeze.

Bruce's throat burns from belting out "Drunk on You." His head is reeling. His hands are sweating. He is leaning toward Gary, toward his warmth, his smell. His lips are hot and moist.

And then he falls over, his forehead striking the horn on the steering wheel. The sudden blaring jolts them both up straight. Gary bursts out laughing. "Man, you are *so* fucking drunk." He opens the door and staggers out, and Bruce manages to follow.

Gary heads up the steps to his front door. "See ya tomorrow, man," he says. "Right now I gotta piss like a son-va-bitch."

Bruce watches him go inside, then turns and heads toward his trailer. Above him, the stars are trying to pierce through the pink haze over the city. Bruce shivers in his thin jacket. His feet crunch on the new frost on the grass. "Here, kitty kitty," he calls. But the cat does not come.

SIX

1

Ham shivers. He is sitting in his underwear on an examination table, waiting for Ray. He has been here now for ten minutes, and goose flesh has begun to prickle his arms and legs.

He told Christina yesterday that he was going in to the doctor this morning. She seemed pleased. "I've been worried about you," she told him. "I'll feel better if you get yourself checked out."

But he is worried about her, too. Since Saturday she has been distant, preoccupied. Tense. Like she is keeping something from him. And that is not like her. He considers the idea that she may be bored and restless with their relationship; maybe she wants out. Maybe she is already seeing someone else.

His thoughts are interrupted as Ray knocks on the door and steps into the room. "Sorry I'm so behind," he says. "Had an emergency early this morning."

"That's all right," Ham says. "How are you?"

Ray nods, looking over Ham's chart. "Fine." He looks up at him. "Your blood pressure's kind of high—one-seventy over ninety-five. Does any other doctor treat you for that?"

Ham shakes his head. "It's never been high before."

"Are you nervous?" Ray asks him, and Ham shudders as he remembers his father's nurse asking Dad the same question.

Ham gives a dry laugh. "No more than usual."

Ray nods and sets the chart down. "Well, let's get down to it," he says. He proceeds probing and prodding, touching and feeling. "Experiencing any pain anywhere?"

"No."

"Any dizziness?"

"No."

"Discomfort when you void?"

"No." Void. What a term.

"Any sexual dysfunction? Trouble or discomfort with erection or ejaculation?"

"No."

"What about your diet? Do you eat healthy?" Ray grins. "I know you drink a lot of coffee and wine."

Ham smiles. "I eat pretty well. Christina's into gourmet cooking, you know. *Light* gourmet cooking. Healthy stuff. Olive oil, steamed vegetables, broiled meat. You know."

Ray nods. "That sounds good." He takes a seat in front of him. "Well. I think that about covers all your physical ailments. You're in good shape for a man your age—*our* age." He looks down at the chart, not meeting Ham's eyes. "Let's talk about your depression."

"All right."

"How long's it been going on?"

Ham takes a breath. "Since Jill died."

Ray looks up. "Ham, that's been two years."

"I know."

"Why didn't you come to me before now?"

Ham shakes his head. "I thought it would go away. I thought it was just me trying to get over Jill."

"Two years is a long time," Ray says. He writes something on Ham's chart. "I want to do a blood test," he says. "I want to rule out any kind of thyroid problem." He looks at him squarely. "But I think I'm safe in saying that you have what's called a major depressive disorder—MDD for short."

"What's that?"

"It's a fancy way of saying you have a chemical imbalance in your brain that affects your moods. You see, the brain releases certain. . . compounds in response to certain activities. Serotonin is one of the chemicals that makes you feel good. In MDD, the serotonin is inhibited from being released, and that results in chronic depression."

Ham looks at the floor. "How do you know it's not just grief over Jill?"

"Two years, Ham," Ray says. "That's way too long for transitional depression. Are you sure you never felt depressed before Jill died?"

Ham shrugs. "I don't know. Could be. I mean, I never thought of myself as being happy."

Ray sits back. "See?"

"But I never thought I was *unhappy* either. Not all the time. I guess I've just been sort of. . . apathetic all my life. Except when there's a crisis. Then I get depressed." He blows out a breath. "My brother's conviction was a big blow. And my mother's death."

Ray looks at him. "Did the charges against Bruce depress you?"

"Yes."

"Why?"

"Because it was so damn stupid. *He* was so damned stupid. There was no reason for such a thing to happen." Ham looks at the floor. "And then my mother died right after."

Ray looks at him. "Do you blame Bruce for your mother's death?"

Ham struggles to meet Ray's eyes. No one has ever asked him that before. In fact, he has never thought of it himself. "It was hard on her," he says, but it comes out as a whisper.

"You didn't answer my question, Ham."

Ham looks back at the floor. "Yeah. I guess in a way I do." He glances at Ray. "Do you think that's what's causing my depression?"

"Not really. Most of the time it's not an event that triggers MDD; it's usually just genetics."

"But my parents weren't depressed," Ham says.

Ray shrugs. "Sometimes it stays dormant through a few generations. Kind of like cancer. We know certain types of cancer runs in families. Sometimes it skips a generation. No one knows why. It's much the same for depression."

Ham sighs. "So what happens now?"

"First the blood test. Then we have four different routes we can take." He holds up a finger as he names each one. "First, there's psychotherapy. Then chemotherapy—medication, in other words. Then electro-shock therapy. And finally, some kind of combination."

Ham stares at the wall. *Electro-shock therapy*. All he can picture is Jack Nicholson in *One Flew over the Cuckoo's Nest*, biting hard on a leather strap and convulsing while electricity shoots through him. "What do you suggest?"

"Psychotherapy alone takes too long—sometimes years—before you can see any results. Electro-shock therapy isn't used much anymore; in fact, it's hardly ever used even for the most severe cases."

Ham manages a dry chuckle. "I was worried about that one."

"Well, it's not nearly as violent as the movies make it out to be," Ray says, smiling. "But the most popular method right now for treating depression is simple medication. I've had several patients who have done very well on anti-depressants."

Ham chews the inside of his jaw. "But won't that just cover up my feelings? Surely that wouldn't solve the problem."

Ray shrugs. "Depends. I know some people who have been able to tackle their problems and solve them after being on medication for awhile. It depends on the individual and how much he or she wants to change."

"You mentioned something about a combination of treatments."

Ray nods. "Because in some patients the medication tends to simply mask the symptoms, like you were concerned about, I'll suggest using chemotherapy along with psychotherapy. Talking to a good counselor can help you change your negative thinking and affect your behavior. In other words, the medication helps you feel better while you learn how to live without it."

Ham looks at him. "So if I go on medication, I

probably won't have to be on it the rest of my life."

Ray shrugs. "Again, it depends on the individual." He scribbles on a green prescription pad, then tears off the paper and gives it to Ham. "Get this filled. Take two of these capsules each morning. I'd like you to stick with the medication for a month, then come back and see me. Then we'll decide if you need to see a counselor, too. In the meantime, we'll go ahead and do the blood test, and if we see there is a problem with your thyroid, I'll give you call."

Ham nods, looking at the prescription. "Okay."

"By the way," Ray says, "that medicine's expensive, so I hope your insurance is paid up. I know what tightwads you bankers are."

Ham gives him a smile, then claps him on the shoulder. "Thanks, Ray."

2

Christina is loading the dishwasher in Ham's kitchen. Kipp is out, gone somewhere in his car, and she feels relieved. They have hardly spoken since Saturday, and when they have, Christina notices Kipp doesn't meet her eyes. She doesn't know what to do. She hates to tell Ham for fear of being a stool-pigeon, of betraying Kipp. But then it's Ham's right to know his kid is smoking dope.

She latches the dishwasher and turns it on, then heads for the door to the garage. Ham is working on another project—an old bookcase. He is stripping the ancient paint and lacquer off the wood, and the chemical fumes sting Christina's eyes as she steps down and leans back against Ham's workbench.

He turns and looks at her. "Hi."

"Hi. How's it going?"

He shrugs. "All right, I guess." His fingers are black and stained with old varnish. "Solid oak under here," he tells her.

She watches his back as he works, as the muscles strain beneath his old ragged polo shirt, just above the collar where his dark gray hair curls around his tanned neck. God, she loves this man. She shoves her hands into the pockets of her jeans. "Ham, I love you."

He turns and looks at her. "I love you, too, honey." He gives her a crooked smile and goes back to his work.

"I don't know exactly how to say this," she says, and she sees him stiffen. "But please understand. . . " Her voice cracks.

He turns back to her. "What is it, Chris?"

She feels her eyes fill with tears. "Please understand I wouldn't tell you this if I didn't love you so much."

Ham is standing, looking at her, not moving. "What is it?" he says again.

She looks at the floor, her hand covering her face. "Saturday. . . while you were playing golf. . . when I came over to fix lunch. . . " She looks at him. "I accidentally walked in on Kipp. He was smoking pot."

Ham breaks his gaze and looks away. "Great," he says.

"I didn't want to tell you," she is saying, "but I thought you should know."

"It's okay, honey." He moves to hug her, and then he laughs, and his voice is filled with humor. "I thought you were going to leave me," he says.

She looks up at him, puzzled. "What in the world made you think that?"

"You'd been so moody the past couple of days, I

just knew something was wrong."

"I just didn't know how to tell you," she says. "I was so shocked. I didn't know what to say."

"It's all right," he tells her, then he lets out a breath. "I guess I'd better talk to him about it." He picks up a greasy rag and wipes his hands with it. "But hell, I smoked grass when I was young. Everybody did." He looks at her. "*You* did."

She looks away. "I know. But I'm not proud of it." She feels bitter when she thinks of those dark days. Those days with Kevin. And she supposes in a way that Kevin is to her what Bruce is to Ham—an embarrassment, an indelible black spot that cannot be scrubbed away, like the bloodstains Lady Macbeth vainly tried to wash out. She glances back at him. "But drugs are different now. They're. . . I don't know, more powerful. And we know more about how dangerous they are than we did back then."

Ham stoops over. "Back in my day," he says in his best old geezer voice, "grass was grass. We smoked what we had, and we didn't complain that it wasn't strong enough."

Christina has to laugh. "C'mon, Ham. I'm serious."

He pulls her close to him. "Okay, honey. I'll talk to him about it."

"I feel like a tattle-tale. I feel like I'm butting in."

Ham kisses her neck. "You sound like a mother."

3

Kipp pulls his Mazda up into the drive. Good. Christina's not here.

All evening he has been driving through town, endlessly circling the main streets, the residential sections, the choppy subdivision lanes. Anything to avoid going home. Anything to avoid Christina.

God, she was shocked. He almost laughs when he thinks of the expression on her face. And he would have laughed if he hadn't have been so goddamned mad.

He unlocks the door and steps into the darkness. Ham must already be in bed. The house is quiet. Like a tomb. He moves through the den toward the hallway.

"Kipp."

He jumps, whirling toward the voice. "Jesus, Dad, you scared the shit outa me."

"Don't swear, Kipp." Ham is sitting in his recliner, and Kipp can barely see the outline of his head in the blackness. "Sit down."

Kipp feels his way to the sofa. "I thought you were already in bed."

"I was sitting here dozing. Waiting for you."

Kipp pulls off his jacket. Ham is scaring him. It's like some scene from an old gangster movie. "Why are you in the dark?"

"Sorry." Ham switches on a lamp, and they both squint in the sudden light. "I need to talk to you."

Shit, Kipp thinks. "What about?" he asks, trying to make his voice light.

Ham is rubbing his forehead. He is holding a half-empty bottle of beer. "Christina told me what happened Saturday."

Kipp blows out a breath. What a bitch. He looks away. "So what did she say?"

Ham takes a deep breath. "She said she found you smoking pot in your room."

Kipp glares at him. "Well, did she tell you she came barging in there without knocking?"

"I don't think she did it on purpose, Kipp."

Kipp flops back against the couch. "I'm not so sure."

Ham's face is red. "That's not the point, son."

Kipp stares at the wall. "Then what is the point, Dad? I'm tired. I'd like to go to bed."

"The point is, what the hell were you doing smoking pot?"

Kipp rolls his eyes. "C'mon, Dad. Get real. It's only *weed* for chrissakes. It's not like it's coke or anything."

"Do you know how easy it is to step over the line, to get into the harder stuff after you've been smoking pot?"

"Oh, please, Dad." Kipp laughs. "That's so ridiculous."

"Is it?"

"Yes." He looks at Ham. "I'm not stupid. I'm not gonna get into coke or meth or any of that shit."

"How do you know that?"

"Please."

"Stop saying that." Ham swipes his fingers through his sweaty hair. "You just don't know. You think it can't happen to you. You think you're invincible."

"I don't think that."

"Then stop. For God's sake, Kipp. I don't want you to end up with a bad drug problem."

"I won't."

His father sighs and leans his head against the back of the chair, looking at the beams in the ceiling. "This is going nowhere. We're both tired." He looks at him. "I just want you to know that I'm concerned, Kipp. I don't want you on drugs. For your safety. For your health. I don't want you to hurt yourself. I want you to be informed. I want you to know what that crap can do to your body."

Kipp stares at the blank television screen. "Can I go to bed now?"

Ham closes his eyes, rubbing his temples. "Yes. Just please think about what I've said."

Kipp grabs his jacket and heads down the hall toward his room. Shit. Everyone's so fucking concerned about him. Why can't they just leave him alone? Why can't they just let him have some peace?

4

Bruce has just finished a burrito. He scrapes the last of the sauce off the plate with his fork and shovels it into his mouth. The late news has just come on, and he watches for a moment before climbing to his feet to take his dishes to the kitchen sink.

The cat has begun to get friendly with him. The past couple of days, when Bruce has stepped outside to fill up the bowl with food, it has rubbed around his legs, meowing. The cat makes him feel good, like someone needs him. He should name it, he thinks.

He piles the plate and fork in the sink and rinses them off. He does not have to go in to work tonight, and he is glad. He is tired. His body aches with fatigue. Last night was rough. Just as he went on his shift, the basketball game at the county high school ended, and the store was teeming with customers—people getting gas, Cokes, cigarettes. It was two hours before he could even catch his breath. By then he was sweating profusely, and the underarms and back of his blue smock were soaked through.

As tired as he was this morning when his shift

ended, though, as soon as Kelly came through the door, his spirits soared. His body suddenly pumped up with adrenaline. He is falling in love. He feels good when he sees her. Just seeing her is almost enough.

Bruce jumps as someone knocks on the door. Outside, Gary stands on the steps, a cigarette dangling from his lips. He grins and holds up a DVD. "Got something for us," he says.

Bruce looks at it. *Bi Girls in Heat*. Gary is always bringing over porno movies, rented from the video place down the street. "Pop it in," he says, nodding toward the TV.

Gary kneels in front of the television and loads the disc. "Got any beer?"

"Sure." Bruce pulls two bottles from the refrigerator and twists off the caps. "Bud Light okay?"

"Yeah." Gary takes his beer and sinks into the couch, his eyes glued to the screen.

Bruce sits down in his chair, watching him. Sometimes Gary masturbates during these movies, rubbing his erection through his jeans. He tries to hide it, but Bruce knows. Sometimes Bruce masturbates the same way while he watches Gary. He clears his throat. "We need to go bar-hopping again soon."

Gary glances at him, nodding. "Yeah. We had fun."

Bruce takes a sip of beer. It is his third tonight, and his head is beginning to buzz. The movie blazes on. The opening shot is of a guy and a girl screwing on a pool table. "Oh, oh, oh," she is screaming as the guy grunts in reply. The camera zooms in until the couple's genitalia fill the screen. Suddenly, another woman appears in the room. "What the hell are you doing?" she screams. The couple look at her. "Candy's never been fucked before," she tells them. She pulls the guy away. "Let me show you how she likes it." She kneels between the other girl's legs and begins to lick. The camera zooms in again.

Bruce glances over at Gary. He sits bolt upright in astonishment. Gary is masturbating, his thin penis poking stiffly out of his fly, his hand flying up and down. Bruce immediately has an erection. Quietly, he unzips his jeans and pulls it out, stroking it.

His heart is pounding violently. He can feel the chair shaking with each beat.

And suddenly, he is on his knees beside Gary, and their gazes lock. Bruce bends down and takes Gary into his mouth, his tongue working and working, tasting the salty bitterness of him, one hand stroking himself.

Gary is looking at him dumbly, his eyes wide and glazed, and Bruce thinks, *He's going to come. He's going to come in my mouth.*

And suddenly, the side of Bruce's head explodes in pain. He falls backwards, looking at Gary, at Gary's upraised fist. "You motherfucking *faggot*," Gary hisses.

Bruce's gut is on fire. "But I thought. . ." he croaks.

Gary stands, stuffing his wilting penis back into his jeans. "You thought what?" he spits. "That I'm queer?"

Bruce rolls over, covering his eyes with his arm. He is crying, and he doesn't want Gary to see him crying. "I'm sorry," he says.

"You pathetic son-of-a-bitch," Gary says. "A fucking queer. You're a goddamned *queer*." And then his foot swings down – *hard*—into Bruce's side. "You sick fuck."

Bruce clutches his abdomen. "Please. Stop." Gary's foot comes down again. Bruce loses his breath. All he can do is hold himself, the pain screaming inside him.

And then Gary's shoe strikes him between the legs, and he goes numb at first. And then the excruciating, nauseating pain creeps up his belly. He writhes on the floor, clutching his testicles, drawing his knees up to his chest. And then the vomit spews forth. The remains of that damned burrito.

Gary crouches beside him. "You ever come near me again I'll cut your cock off." He storms out, leaving the door banging in the crisp breeze. It flops open, catches on the spring and bangs closed, then opens again.

Bruce lies gasping for breath on the floor, the worn carpet like sandpaper against his face. His face is streaked with tears. His belly is hard as he bears down against the pain in his groin.

Behind him, the door bangs shut, swings open, catches on the spring, bangs shut, swings open. . . .

SEVEN

1

Hamilton Senior is sitting in the front seat of the car like a mannequin. His gaze never shifts from the road in front of them. He's scared, Ham thinks, glancing at him.

Ham tightens his grip on the steering wheel. *This is my father and he is dying.* Part of him resents his father for this, for becoming weak and sick and forcing Ham to take time from work to haul him to doctors; and immediately, as the thoughts enter his mind, he is pummeled by sickening guilt.

Bruce should be here, Ham thinks; Bruce should be here helping me with all this shit.

There are times when Ham feels a true, burning hatred for Bruce, and this is one of them. To Ham's knowledge, Bruce has not called to check on their father in almost ten years. Bruce should have the courtesy to at least call Dad and see how he's doing. Even if he won't help. Even if he won't lift a finger for

Dad, he should at least call him. Sometimes it would be better if Bruce had never been born. Ham's responsibilities certainly wouldn't be any less, but his worries might be.

But then there are times when a flicker of hatred ignites for his father, too. When he thinks of the past, of times when he despised Hamilton Senior.

One of those times was when Ham was eight years old. He was an only child then and short for his age. His mother pitied him, he thinks, but whether it was because of his size or his loneliness, he was never sure. But he had few friends. Most of it, he believes, was because of his father's wealth. Moving in the social circles of the city's affluent families, Ham was aware that most of those kids were extremely popular; they attended private schools (the most prestigious being Oak Heights Academy, where Kipp goes now) and exclusive summer camps. Ham went to public high school because his father refused to flaunt his wealth; sending Ham to a private academy would have been "vulgar." But in public school, Ham was downright hated by his classmates. As a result, he was never able to feel comfortable with either the wealthy kids or the middle-class kids. One group looked down on him for going to public school; the other thought him to be a rich snob.

It all came together for him one day at his father's country club. A father and son shooting match, open to the public. Hamilton Senior had entered them in the competition just for the fun of it, even though Ham had hardly ever touched a gun.

It was a crisp, late winter morning, the kind of morning when even the hills farthest away stand out in sharp detail in the early sun. Ham knew most of the other boys there, and they were from both circles. His heart hammered as he recognized a few whose athletic prowess was well-regarded. Ham had never been sports-minded; baseball, football—they all bored him. Movies and science kept his interest. And books, especially classics like *Treasure Island* and *Huck Finn*. But an intellectual twelve-year-old has a tendency to grow plump and slow, and Ham's weight had skyrocketed since last summer. Now he moved with the ungraceful, self-conscious ballet that fat boys seem to possess, and the worst of it was that they—all of them gathered here—would be watching. And, though he tried to tell himself he imagined it, they were waiting for him to screw up.

Ham stood with his father and watched the first few boys and their dads demolish their clay pigeons. He watched as the boys took aim, following the pigeons' rise into the air, and then blasted them out of the sky.

And then it was Ham's turn, and he stepped forward to the shooting area. His father knelt behind him. The steel of the trigger was icy-cold against his finger. "Whenever you're ready, son," Hamilton Senior told him.

Ham looked at the blue horizon, at the gray-green hills in the distance. Behind him, he could hear the men and their sons shuffling on their feet and his father's ragged breathing. The barrel of his shotgun wavered with each heartbeat; they were all looking at him, he knew. He could feel their gaze boring into his head. "*Pull!*" he screamed, and his voice cracked in the cold air.

The clay pigeon soared toward the clouds, and Ham tried to follow it the way the other boys had.

"Now," he heard his father whisper. The pigeon began to descend. "Now!" Hamilton Senior barked. "Shoot, Ham!"

Ham squeezed the trigger, and the shot exploded in his ears. The butt slammed against his shoulder, knocking him backwards into his father. "Did I hit it?" he cried.

"No," Hamilton Senior told him flatly, and some of the men behind them laughed. "You've got two more chances."

Ham's face was burning with embarrassment. He reloaded the gun and took his stance. "Pull!"

This time his finger flexed as soon as he saw the pigeon. The gun fired. The pigeon flew on.

"No, no, dammit!" his father cried. "Too soon." He grabbed the shotgun from his hands and ejected the spent shell. "You've got to wait until you've got the right aim." He shoved the new shell into the barrel and thrust it at Ham. "This is your last chance."

Ham lifted the gun before him. It was shaking again. His ears were on fire, and he was sure, even under his cap, that everyone behind him could see how he was blushing, how he was trembling. "Pull," he said. Nothing happened.

"They didn't hear you, Ham," his father said.

"Pull!"

The pigeon flew into the air. Ham watched it in the gun sight, following its arc across the sky. He pulled the trigger, this time bracing his shoulder against the butt. "I got it!" he cried. The men behind them laughed.

His father pulled the gun from his hands. "No, you missed again. We're out of it."

Ham followed Hamilton Senior through the crowd,

not looking at anyone. The boys were laughing. He had failed. He had embarrassed himself in front of all the men. Worse, he had embarrassed his father.

Hamilton Senior shook his head at the others. "Damn waste of a ten-dollar entry fee," he spat.

* * *

The hospital looms before them, stark and cold and immense. "Here we are," he says.

Hamilton Senior is small and shriveled in the seat beside him. "Will Dr. Steinfield be there?"

Ham nods his head. "Yeah. He'll take the tissue sample and send it on to the lab."

His father watches the building as they pull into the parking lot. "I dread this," he says.

Ham turns off the engine. "I know."

"Promise me, something."

"What, Dad?"

His father looks at him. "Don't let me die here. I don't want to die in the hospital."

Ham sighs, staring ahead at a plump woman in a blue dress climbing into a maroon Lincoln Town Car. "It's just a test, Dad. You're not going to die."

"Just promise me, son," he says again.

Ham nods, looking at him. "Okay."

2

It has been three days since the biopsy.

Early yesterday afternoon, Dr. Steinfield called Ham at work and asked him to come in today. Christina saw how shaken Ham was last night, and it frightens her somehow. He did not eat any dinner; he simply sat in the dark den, watching the night through the bay window, drinking a bottle of Chianti.

Christina brought her own glass and joined him on

the sofa. "Can I have a sip?"

Ham grunted and poured her glass half-full. "Good stuff," he said, his voice thick.

Christina watched him sipping from the mouth of the bottle, something she had never seen him do. "Are you all right, babe?"

He looked at her, his dark blue eyes barely visible in the dim light. "I'm okay."

"Are you taking your medicine?"

"Yeah." He took a drink of wine. "Ray says it might be a coupla weeks before I notice any change."

She reached out for his hand. "I love you."

He smiled thinly. "I love you, too."

And now, here they sit in Dr. Steinfield's office, with Hamilton Senior on the far side of Ham. Ham holds Christina's hand tightly, and she can see his knuckles turning white.

Steinfield looks at them, at Ham's father. "The results of the test aren't too good, I'm afraid," he says.

Hamilton Senior sits up straight. "It's malignant, isn't it?" he says.

Steinfield looks at him and nods. "Yes. And the blood samples we took indicate that the cancer may have spread."

Ham's hand tightens on Christina's. He's going to break my hand, she thinks. "What happens now?" Ham asks.

Steinfield blows out a breath. "We need to do a bone scan and several other tests to know for certain whether the cancer has spread."

"What do you think?" Hamilton Senior says.

Steinfield looks at him. "Based on what I've seen so far, I'd say there's an eighty-percent chance the cancer has invaded some other organs."

Ham's father stares at the floor. "Then that would mean it's. . ."

"Terminal," Steinfield finishes for him. He looks at them. "I know this is not easy. It's not easy for me, either. The best thing to do is go ahead and get the tests over with; at least then we'll know for certain."

"When do you want to do that?" Ham asks.

"I'd like to go ahead and admit him today, do the tests this week."

Christina tries to avoid looking at Ham, but she sees the shiny hint of tears in his eyes. She forces herself to look away, to study the Remington sculpture on Steinfield's bookcase, a cowboy on the back of a horse. The horse is rearing on its back legs; below it lies a rattlesnake, poised to strike.

* * *

At two o'clock, after Hamilton Senior is settled into a room, Christina and Ham leave the hospital, heading across town for home. Ham looks exhausted; his eyes are puffy and his face is lined and pale. "Why don't you take a nap when you get home," she suggests.

He nods, watching the traffic ahead. "I hated to leave him there," he says.

"I know."

"But he just insisted that we leave."

"He'll be all right, Ham. He probably would like some time to himself."

Ham slows for a truck to turn off the road in front of them. "I guess I should call Bruce."

3

Sixth period.

Kipp is sitting in algebra class, watching that prick Mills pace back and forth in front of the blackboard.

He is pointing to a problem he has scrawled out and explaining how to work it.

Kipp glances over at Sherrie Cotton. She is wearing a light-blue denim jumper with bears on the front, and she has a white lace ribbon wound in her dark hair. She is sitting at rapt attention, her gaze not shifting from Mills. Probably wants to fuck him, Kipp thinks; probably would fuck anything that walks from what he has heard. *She* would probably give him a blow-job. And she would probably like it. She would probably drain him dry. He smiles as he feels an erection straining against the fly of his jeans.

He hasn't talked to Amber in days. She hasn't spoken to him in school, and he refuses to call or even text her. Let the bitch suffer. She still hasn't changed her relationship status on Facebook, but he supposes it's over between them and he may as well start looking for someone else. That's fine with him. Just less bullshit he'll have to put up with.

Brett, on the other hand, slid in beside him at lunch today, a half-eaten bag of Fritos in his hand. "How's it going, man?" he asked, his mouth full.

Kipp looked at him as he pulled off a bite of lunchroom pizza with his front teeth. "Fine."

"Bunch of us going over to Mark Thomas' tonight. Should be pretty wild. You wanna go?"

Kipp shrugged. "Maybe."

"Text me if you want me to pick you up."

"Sure."

Brett looked at him. "Hey, when you coming back to practice? You're not quitting, are you?"

"Don't know. Murphy hasn't told me I could come back."

Brett raised his eyebrows. "No shit?"

Kipp looked back at his pizza. "Guess he's waiting to see how my algebra grades look. Maybe he's waiting on a report from Mills."

Brett shook his head. "Those two have it in for you, man," he said. "That's a bad deal."

Kipp glanced at him. Finally, there seemed to be someone on his side. Brett wasn't such a bad guy after all. Maybe Brett was even right about Amber. Hell, girls come and go, but a guy needs his best friend. "Maybe I *will* go with you tonight," he told Brett.

Suddenly, he is again aware that he is sitting in algebra class. Everyone is looking at him. Mills is looking at him. "Did you hear me, Mr. Bradford?"

Kipp blinks. "I'm sorry. What did you say?"

Mills points at the problem on the board. "I asked you to tell me how to work this."

Kipp stares at the equation. $2(x + 2x—4y)=6y$. He swallows. Fuck.

"Do you know how to begin, Mr. Bradford?"

What a prick, Kipp thinks, not looking at him. "First," he says, "you multiply two times x and $2x$ and $4y$. . ."

Mills is shaking his head. "Wrong. Don't you remember the rules for solving equations?"

Kipp looks at him dumbly, thinking, *You prick, you prick, you motherfucking prick*. "I guess not," he says, trying to keep his voice even.

"Parenthetical work first," Mills reminds him.

Kipp clears his throat and looks back at the board. He can feel his face burning. "Add x and $2x$ and subtract the $4y$?"

Mills stuffs his hands in his pockets. "Can you subtract a y from an x?"

Kipp blows out a breath, looking at the ceiling.

"No." He licks his lips. "Add x and $2x$ and add $4y$ to both sides."

Mills looks at him. "You're forgetting something."

Kipp stares at the problem. His gut is boiling. He chews his tongue. "What?"

"Don't forget you've got a two sticking out there. What are you going to do with that?"

Kipp takes a deep breath. His whole body is quivering.

"Mr. Bradford? What are you going to do with that two?"

Kipp looks at him. "This is bullshit," he hisses.

Mills blinks, moving closer. "Excuse me?"

Kipp stands, knocking his chair over. "This is just a bunch of bullshit. You're just trying to fuck me over."

The room is deadly silent. Mills moves toward him. "Let's talk in the hall," he mutters.

Kipp is heading for the door. "Fuck you," he says. He storms out, racing down the hall, toward the outside.

Behind him, Mills is running. "Bradford! Kipp!"

Then Kipp emerges into the gray, crisp day, and he can hear him no more.

4

Bruce sits slumped on his stool behind the counter at the Gas-N-Pack. His belly and ribs still hurt from being kicked, and yesterday he noticed the dark bruises were turning deep purple, ringed with yellow-green. He takes shallow breaths, afraid of the pain if he should expand his lungs too much.

God, that was stupid. The dumbest thing he has ever done. Now Gary is convinced that he is queer. Bruce closes his eyes, thinking with embarrassment of the shocked look on Gary's face, the dazed expression in his eyes that Bruce thought – moronically—meant Gary was lost in pleasure.

He hasn't seen Gary since it happened. He hasn't wanted to. He hasn't even looked for him. For a while, he was afraid Gary might come back and attack him again or serve him an eviction notice. He still worries about that, but his fear seems to be subsiding a bit.

He looks at his watch. Six-thirty. The day outside is dawning gray and cold. Some of his regular customers this morning have told him there is snow in the weather forecast, and looking at the dense, black clouds in the sky he can believe it. Funny, he thinks. Last week he was wearing shorts outside and sweating while he played basketball. But that seems like a hundred years ago. Before Gary. B.G.

What is wrong with me? he thinks. Maybe he is queer after all. Maybe he *is* a goddamned pathetic faggot. *Why* did he do that? *Why?* It sickens him now as he thinks of it.

His stomach bottoms out as he sees Kelly's Escort pull into the lot. He glances at his watch; she is early.

Those thoughts of Gary make him want to run to Kelly and lose himself in her arms. He wants to hold onto her, to cling to her. Maybe, he thinks, maybe she will be able to stop the hurt, to end all this confusion.

She steps into the store, her light brown hair settling about her shoulders. "Whoo!" she cries. "It's winter again!"

He smiles. "You're early."

She nods, moving toward the coat closet behind the counter. "Yeah." She pulls off her jacket and hangs it up. "I didn't stay and have coffee with my mom this morning. I just dropped off Amanda and headed on in."

She steps down to the coffee bar. "Great. Fresh java."

"Just made it."

She pours a cup and looks back at him. "Want some?"

He shakes his head. "Nah. It'll just keep me awake."

She adjusts her nametag and sits down on the stool beside him, then blows on her coffee and takes a tentative sip. "You don't look like you feel too good today."

He manages a smile. "Just tired, I guess."

A red Chevy Trailblazer pulls up to the gas pumps, and Bruce recognizes the driver as Paul Nichols, an investment broker at a bank down on Virginia Street. Bruce watches him step out of the truck, pulling his gray coat around him against the cold. "He's early today, too," Bruce comments.

Nichols finishes pumping and trots for the inside. "Cold today," he says, fishing out his wallet.

"Forty dollars," Bruce tells him, punching in the sale. "You're early."

Nichols throws two twenties onto the counter and glances outside. "Thought I'd better go on in today and get caught up. You know the forecast is calling for three inches by this afternoon?"

"That right?" Bruce says. He wonders how much Nichols makes a year. Ninety, a hundred thousand easy. "Have a good one," Bruce tells him.

Nichols heads for the door, shaking his head. "Not looking forward to it."

Bruce watches him climb into the Trailblazer and pull out onto the highway. He wonders if Nichols knows Ham, then thinks that surely he does. All those bankers hobnob together at the country club and the golf course.

"Penny for your thoughts," Kelly says behind him, and he looks around. She smiles. "Guess it's about time for you to close up shop."

Bruce glances at his watch. "Yeah." He opens the register and pulls out his cash drawer. Kelly stretches and opens the safe to take out her money. Bruce watches her sign onto the register. "You want me to stay and help you this morning? It might be busy with the snow coming and all."

She smiles, shaking her head. "No, that's all right. Martha will be here in half an hour. I can handle it 'til then." She looks at him. "I appreciate the offer."

He clears his throat, and before he can stop himself, he says, "You dating anybody now?"

She gives him a faint grin. "No." She turns back to the register.

Bruce watches her. His heart is hammering in his chest now. "You wanna go out?" His voice is about to crack, he thinks. "With me?"

She turns around, facing him. "When?"

His words seem caught in his throat. He coughs. "I don't know. . . Saturday? I'm off that night."

She seems to consider this for a moment, staring at the floor with raised eyebrows. "Sure," she says.

He almost laughs. "You will?"

She smiles. "Yeah."

"You like Mexican food?"

"Love it."

God, he thinks; this is not happening. "I know this really great place," he says, feeling excitement growing in his chest. "They've got these gargantuan margaritas and these great chimichangas."

"That sounds good," she says. "I haven't had

Mexican in a long time." She looks at the ceiling. "I'm sure my mom won't care to keep Amanda."

"Great," he says.

On the way home, he can't help but smile. This is incredible, he thinks. She actually said *yes*.

And then, halfway across town, it hits him: eventually she is going to find out. She will find out why he was in prison and she will cut him off. Freeze him out. They always do. And then he will feel worse than ever.

The cat is hunkered down on his porch when he pulls into the drive. "Hello, kitty," he says, pulling his collar up around his neck. "You cold?"

The cat rubs against his legs. He can feel it purring. He bends down to stroke it between the ears. "You wanna come in? Where it's warm?"

He unlocks the door and holds it open. "C'mon," he says, "c'mon, kitty."

The cat looks at him, then eyes the open door.

"C'mon," Bruce says again.

It gives Bruce one last look and then darts inside, into the dark trailer.

EIGHT

1

Ham eases his door closed and sits down behind his desk, turning his chair to face the window. Outside, light snow has begun to fall, floating down like feathers. The lunchtime traffic eases by on the street; the roads are growing white and slick.

He slips the phone book out of his credenza. It is pathetic that he doesn't know his own brother's telephone number. He runs his finger down the list of names until he finds it. Ham's heart begins to hammer as he picks up the receiver and punches in Bruce's number. He has no idea what he is going to say. He waits for Bruce to answer, his arms folded tightly over his chest.

"Hello?"

"Bruce?"

"Yeah."

"This is Ham."

There is silence on the other end for a moment.

"How are ya?" Bruce says.

"Fine. You?"

"All right."

Ham clears his throat. "I'm calling to let you know that Dad is in the hospital."

"What's the matter?"

"He's having some tests done. He's got prostate cancer, Bruce. The doctor wants to see if it's spread."

Bruce blows out a breath. "How bad?"

"It doesn't look too good." Ham watches an elderly lady trudge by on the sidewalk, her arms loaded with two paper bags of groceries. "It may be terminal."

"Jeez. Is he at the hospital here in town?"

"Yeah. Room three-twenty-one. You need to go see him."

"I know I do," Bruce says, sounding irritated. "How's he doing?"

"All right, I suppose. His spirits are good."

"That's good."

Ham swivels in his chair, turning to stare at the paneled wall. "So how're things with you?"

"I'm okay."

"You still working?"

"Yeah. I'm the night manager at the Gas-N-Pack over by the interstate."

"I know that place," Ham says. *My God*, he thinks, *how pathetic*.

"What's going on with you?" Bruce asks.

"Same old thing."

"How's your little boy?" Bruce laughs. "Not little anymore. I saw him a week or two ago."

"Yeah?"

"He was in the store."

"He's doing well," Ham says, but he is thinking

about the conversation he and Kipp had about pot. "He's doing all right."

"You ever get married again?"

"No," Ham tells him. "Maybe next year. Christina's getting anxious, I think."

"Who?"

"Christina Alexander. Owns Alexander Realty." Ham pushes his chair up to the desk. "Hey, why don't you come over and meet her sometime."

Bruce is silent for a moment. "You mean it?"

"Yeah. We'll have dinner, catch up on things."

"When?"

Ham ponders this for a moment. "How about tonight? I'm sure Christina won't mind."

"You sure?"

"Yeah. I'd like to see you. Maybe after dinner we can go see Dad together."

"I'd like that. What time?"

Ham glances at his watch. Almost one. "I'll leave here at about four-thirty, and then I'm going to run by the hospital, so I should be home about five-thirty. Any time after that."

"Sounds good," Bruce says, and Ham can tell he is pleased. "I'll see you then."

"You remember where I live?"

"Oh, yeah. I won't have any trouble unless it snows three feet."

Ham hangs up the phone and looks at it. Why in God's name did he do that? He doesn't want Bruce at the house. He doesn't want Christina to meet him. And he sure doesn't want Kipp around him. He swivels around to watch the snow outside.

Ham and Bruce were never close, partly because Ham is ten years older. In a sense, they both grew up as only children. In fact, when Ham went away to college, coming home on weekends seemed like returning to find a distant cousin living in his house. Bruce was a rowdy kid, willowy and outgoing— nothing like Ham was at that age, and he supposes that is another reason the two of them have never been close. They were strangers. And still are.

He reaches for the phone again. Better warn Christina.

2

She is nervous.

She stands in the dining room window, watching the snow blanket the street outside. This is her second glass of wine, and she is still jittery. Her breath steams up the glass, and she moves back toward the light of the kitchen to check on the scampi in the oven.

What little Ham has told her of Bruce has not been good. She knows he was convicted of rape, and that's enough for her. My God, she thinks, what if he gets here before Ham does? At least Kipp is here.

She glances toward the den, where the tinny music of Looney Tunes is blaring from the television. Kipp has said one word to her the whole time she has been here: "Hello." She hasn't seen him since, and she wonders if maybe that's for the best. However, it relieves her some to know that he is around, even though he might not be much help against a grown man.

Car lights blaze up the front of the house for a moment, startling her, and she can only stand motionless until she hears the click of the key in the front door. "Chris?" comes Ham's voice, and she realizes she has been holding her breath. "In here," she calls.

He steps in, snow melting into dark wet spots on his gray overcoat. "Hi, honey," he says, kissing her behind the ear. She can smell a slight vestige of his cologne, a hint of perspiration, and it excites her somehow. "Heard from Bruce?" he asks.

"Not yet." She embraces him again. "I'm glad you're home. I've been so nervous all afternoon."

He grunts. "Me too."

She lays her cheek against the wet lapel of his coat. "I was wondering what in the world I would do if he got here before you did. I mean. . . you know."

Ham nods. "Yeah, I know." He nods toward the wine. "Can I have some of that?"

She smiles. "Sure."

He slips off his coat and heads toward the foyer to hang it up. "Looks like you've made a pretty good dent in it."

"This is only my second glass, thank you," she says, feigning indignation. She pours him a glass and hands it to him as he comes back in loosening his tie. "Beaujolais," she says.

She watches him swirl the glass, then tip it back and take a sip. "Good," he says. "Is this the one you picked out last time?" She nods, and he kisses her on the cheek. "Good choice." He glances around. "Where's Kipp?"

"Isn't he in the den? Watching cartoons?"

Ham shakes his head. "I peeked in there just now and he's not there."

Christina moves back toward the stove. "Maybe he's in his room," she says, avoiding Ham's gaze.

"Maybe," he says, and she is relieved when he doesn't go to look for him; she really is not in the mood for a confrontation with Kipp tonight.

An engine roars up in the driveway. "Must be Bruce," Ham says, looking at the floor. He drains his glass and heads for the front door.

Christina busies herself with the rice and vegetables on the stove, her back to the doorway. Her heart is pounding again, and she realizes she has broken into a sweat. She pats the perspiration off her forehead with a dishtowel; she doesn't want to meet Bruce with a drippy face. She can hear them talking in the foyer; Bruce's voice is soft and low. And suddenly, she hears them enter the kitchen.

She is surprised when she sees Ham's brother. He is nothing like Ham. He is short and pudgy with thinning black hair and a sharp nose. And the first thing she thinks is, *He looks like a rat*. All he needs is a set of whiskers. He is wearing a white oxford shirt beneath a ragged multi-colored mohair sweater and a pair of blue chinos that look about two sizes too small for him; his tan suede chukkas are worn black and smooth, wet from walking through the snow. "Hello," she says.

Ham introduces them, and Bruce extends his hand. Christina looks at it for a moment, not wanting to touch him. But before Bruce can feel awkward, she reaches out, fighting the urge to wince as if she is going to touch something repulsive. "Nice to meet you," he says, and she is surprised at how warm and dry his hand is.

"I'm going to show Bruce the house," Ham tells her.

She nods toward the stove. "Dinner's almost ready," she says. She watches them move toward the den, and she feels a slight shiver.

* * *

Christina is not surprised when Kipp doesn't answer her knock on his door to tell him dinner is on the table. Nor is she surprised to find his room locked. She puts her ear to the smooth wood of the door, listening, but she can hear nothing.

Back in the dining room, Ham and Bruce have started eating. "He won't answer," Christina says.

Ham shrugs, shoveling a forkful of scampi into his mouth. "He'll come out when he's hungry," he says, looking at his plate.

Christina pokes at her shrimp; it has become cold and rubbery. "I don't think he's even in there."

"Maybe he's out with Brett."

She sighs. "I suppose he could have left while I was in the kitchen."

Ham nods. "Yeah. Don't worry about him."

Bruce takes a sip of his beer. "Dinner's good, Christina," he says.

Christina gives him a half-smile. "Thank you."

The rest of the meal is eaten in silence.

3

Kipp is sitting in the big oak behind the house, looking through the windows at them, watching them eat. The wind knocks a sputter of snow down his collar, and he pulls his jacket up around his neck.

When he was little, he had a tree house here; his dad tore it down two years ago, right after his mom died. "It's rotten," he told Kipp, but Kipp thinks Ham just wanted to get rid of it. He still sits up here occasionally, wedged between the trunk and a thick limb.

He is looking at Bruce. Bruce looks nervous.

They all look nervous. No one appears to be talking much.

He leans back against the rough bark of the tree. At least he's not in there, pretending to be sociable like the rest of them. What a crock of shit.

The wind is razor-sharp against his cheeks, and his ass feels like an ice-cube. But he is not going inside. Earlier, while Christina was cooking, he sneaked out through the back door in the mud room. He walked right behind Christina and she never even knew it. What a stupid bitch.

He thought about jacking off when he first came out here. He does that sometimes up here in the tree. He'd love to just take it out and really whack it while he watches them, and they would never know they could probably look through the window and see him. But tonight he'd probably freeze his dick off. God, he wishes he'd at least brought a joint out here.

When Kipp was seven years old, he found a dead dachshund out here in the thicket behind the house. Where it came from or how long it had been there, he never knew. But he remembers prodding it with the toe of his sneaker, watching it turn stiffly beneath his foot, its black mouth curled into a grisly sneer. And when he flipped the dog on its back, he found its underside was completely hollow, eaten away by the maggots that still crawled through it. He thought about burying it, about going into the garage and getting his dad's spade and digging a hole out there in the woods; he even went so far as to bring his wagon out to the dog and load it up, maggots and all. But in the end, he pulled the carcass to the overpass just outside of the subdivision and dumped it onto the roadway below, watching it spin until it hit the asphalt. Then he watched until a pickup truck roared over it, crushing it like a walnut shell. Then he walked back home and ate ten powdered sugar doughnuts and washed them down with a glass of chocolate milk, all while watching Cartoon Carnival on channel five.

He feels like that dog sometimes—all hollow and eaten away, like an empty bag of bones. Like if someone turned him over they would see that dead, black, empty space filled with squirming, stinking maggots.

He shifts uncomfortably in the tree, pressing his sudden erection against the scaly bark of the trunk. Thinking about the dog has made him horny; it always does.

4

Dinner is over, and the three of them have gathered in the den. Ham and Christina are finishing off their wine, and Bruce is working on his second beer. The room is silent. Ham props his feet up on the sturdy coffee table. "We can go on to see Dad whenever you're ready," he tells Bruce.

Bruce takes a swallow of beer. "You don't have to go with me," he says.

Ham looks at him. "You sure?"

Bruce nods. "Yeah. The roads are pretty bad. There's no sense in you getting out if you don't have to."

"I don't care to go."

"I know." Bruce drains his beer and plops the bottle on the table. He looks at them. "Guess I'll go on then."

Ham follows him to the door. "Glad you came over."

Bruce looks back toward Christina. "Dinner was great. Thanks."

"See you," she calls.

Ham and Bruce step out onto the porch. "You have a coat?" Ham asks.

"Didn't wear one," Bruce says. "Hardly ever do."

The snow is falling thick and heavy. The street is covered. "Be careful," Ham says, looking at it.

"Which room you say he was in?

"Three-twenty-one."

Bruce nods, heading for his car. "See ya."

"Yeah."

Bruce climbs into his Nissan and starts up the engine, then rubs his hands together. They are tingling with cold. He turns on the wipers, clearing the snow off the windshield, and he can see that Ham has gone inside and turned out the porch light. Bruce wonders what Ham and Christina are thinking about him, saying about him. Carefully, he backs out of the driveway and heads down the snow-covered street.

Ham certainly didn't seem too keen on Bruce staying around; he practically said it was time for him to go. What a crock of bullshit this whole evening has been. Bruce wonders if Kipp stayed out of sight tonight so he wouldn't have to see him. It's possible.

He wonders what Ham would say if he could see Bruce's trailer. Probably wouldn't expect anything else.

Walking into Ham's house was like walking into an issue of *Architectural Digest*. Everything was perfect. Not a speck of dust anywhere. Even dinner was flawless—not one grain of rice out of place. The perfect house. The perfect woman. The perfect job. Just the perfect life.

For Bruce, growing up in Ham's shadow, it had not been a secret that their father had favored Ham. Everything Bruce did was compared to how Ham had done it. Ham had better manners than Bruce did; Ham hadn't ridden his bike recklessly the way Bruce rode his; Ham hadn't stampeded through the house the way Bruce did. On and on. And even though Dad hadn't said the way Bruce did things was *wrong*, Bruce still heard the disapproval in his father's tone. Ham had been perfect, and there was no way Bruce could have lived up to that.

Bruce blows out a breath as he creeps onto the highway. He supposes that even his conviction had not come as a surprise to their father. In fact, he had never even suggested that he thought Bruce was innocent.

Looking back, he knows that his mother was the only one who ever gave a damn about him. The only one who stood by him, who maintained that she believed his side of the story. But she is dead. And it seemed that all his hopes, his intentions for his life, had died with her.

But that was before Kelly. He thinks of her now, and excitement sparks in his gut and blooms into his chest. When he thinks of how it would be to touch her, to run his hands over her skin, his fingertips almost tingle with the sensation. His lips can almost taste hers pressing against them. His arms can almost feel her body writhing beneath him. His ears can almost hear her whisper, "Let's make love."

But then he realizes that is something he will never hear. He will never touch her or feel her against him. Never. And he supposes that's the reason that drove him to do what he did to Gary the other night. Sheer desperation to just fill that empty space. And maybe, at this point, it doesn't matter whether it's filled by a man or a woman. As long as it's filled. As long as he has someone to hold.

But he doesn't want to be gay, goddammit. He doesn't. If there were just a switch to turn off these feelings. If something as simple as making love to a woman could change him overnight. If one kiss from a princess could change him from a frog.

He eases into the hospital parking lot, peering up at the building. With its floodlights and all the snow, it looks like the hotel in *The Shining*. He pulls at the collar of his sweater; he is sweating, and he realizes for the first time that he is nervous. But why shouldn't he be? After all, this is the first time he's seen his father in since he got out of prison eight years ago.

The cold air feels good as he heads toward the front doors and the new snow crunches beneath his boots. Inside, the lobby is deserted; all of the visitors have gone home to hibernate from the weather.

He takes the elevator to the third floor, then follows the signs toward the west wing. And suddenly, he sees it, and he is standing outside the door. A single placard on the wall, written crudely with a black marker, reads: **BRADFORD, H.** The door is ajar. Bruce peeks in.

A single fluorescent lamp illuminates his father on the bed. *My God*, Bruce thinks, *he's dead*. The blotchy red skin of Hamilton Senior's face is stretched tautly over the bones, and his cheeks and eyes are sunken and dark. Then he sees the chest rise and fall, and Bruce knows his father is only sleeping.

He slips inside and eases into the chair beside the bed, not taking his gaze off the shriveled form. His father's hands grip the blanket, looking like a bird's claws.

Bruce's eyes are burning, and he is struggling to blink back tears. He watches his father's slack, open mouth as it seems to struggle to pull in air and push it back out; it is gray and dry inside. Bruce looks away finally, sickened.

He can't believe this is his father. This tiny, shriveled thing is his *father*. He looks as though he could simply snap into pieces like rotting driftwood.

Bruce almost gasps as he sees his father's eyelids flutter and finally open. The eyes search the ceiling, then dart toward him. His father looks at him. "B—Bruce? Is that my Bruce?"

Bruce moves to the edge of Hamilton Senior's bed. "It's me, Dad."

His father sits up and Bruce embraces him, wincing; he can feel every bone in his father's shoulders, every rib in his back. "How are you doing?"

Hamilton Senior lies back in the bed. "Feel pretty weak," he says. "Just don't have any strength. Doctor talks like it's pretty bad."

Bruce nods gravely. "That's what Ham told me."

His father looks at him. "How are you, son?"

Bruce manages a faint smile. "I'm all right."

"Where you working now?"

"Gas-N-Pack. Over by the interstate. I'm a night manager."

Hamilton Senior nods. "You married yet?"

"No."

"Seeing anybody?"

"Sort of."

His dad laughs weakly. "That's my Bruce. 'Sort of.' You haven't changed a bit."

Bruce looks at his round belly. "Put on some

weight."

"Yeah. You look good, though. Healthy."

"I feel like a pig."

His father blows out a breath. "Nah. You look like a million bucks."

Bruce stares at the floor. "I'm sorry I haven't been to see you."

"It's all right."

"No," says Bruce, shaking his head, "I feel awful about it. I should have come to see you sooner."

"Don't worry about it," his father says. His words are soft and slurred.

"Are you tired?" Bruce asks.

His father nods. His eyelids are already drooping again "That. . . damned pill they gimme. . . "

Bruce stands and puts his hand on his father's bony shoulder. "You rest," he says. "I'll come back tomorrow and see you."

Hamilton Senior nods, and before Bruce can look away, his father is asleep. Bruce looks at his watch; he has only been here ten minutes.

NINE

1

They are all gathered in Hamilton Senior's hospital room—Ham, Christina and Bruce. Ham and Bruce do not meet each other's gaze. Their father lies silently on the bed, watching Dr. Phil on the TV, the sound turned off. Christina stares out the narrow window at the parking lot; there has been no more snow since the other night, and where the lot has been scraped clean by the road crews, the melting snow has created a skating rink. Ham watches her and wonders what she is thinking.

"What time is it?" Hamilton Senior asks.

Ham looks at his watch. "Ten-thirty."

His dad grunts. "Dr. Steinfield was supposed to be here at ten."

Ham blows out a breath. "I know, Dad. He must've had something come up."

"It's not fair to keep a man waiting like this."

"I know."

"When they're coming in to tell you if you're gonna live or die, it's just not fair."

"I know." Ham leans back in his chair and stares at the ceiling panels. His father is nervous. Hell, they're all nervous. Ham feels like he's going to jump through his skin.

He looks at Bruce. Bruce looks sick.

He still can't believe how much weight Bruce has gained. He used to be so skinny, and now he looks like he weighs at least two-fifty. Ham feels sorry for him in a way; Bruce looks miserable. Ham wonders what Bruce's girlfriend looks like; Bruce told him the other night that he was "sort of" seeing someone, and Ham wonders what kind of woman would be interested in a pudgy ex-con. He wonders if she knows that Bruce raped someone; what kind of woman would date a convicted rapist?

There is a knock on the door, and Dr. Steinfield slips in, wiping the sweat from his forehead with the sleeve of his white lab coat. "Sorry I'm late," he says. "Emergency."

Hamilton Senior takes a deep breath. "Let's get down to it," he says, looking at the doctor squarely.

Steinfield crosses his feet and leans back against the wall, flipping through Hamilton Senior's chart. "It's not good," he says, looking around at everyone. "The tests show that the cancer's invaded the bones of your hips. It's also in your kidneys."

Hamilton Senior nods, looking down at the white sheet. "I thought as much."

"Is there anything that can be done?" Bruce asks.

Steinfield chews his lip. "Not really. We can start some radiation to see if that would shrink the cancer, or to see if it would keep it from spreading any farther."

He looks at Ham's father. "But you would have to understand that it's not a cure. It would give you some more time, but it wouldn't get rid of the cancer. The damage is far too extensive for that."

Hamilton Senior purses his lips. "So basically you're telling me I'm gonna die."

Steinfield takes a deep breath. "I'm sorry, Mr. Bradford. This is not easy."

Ham's father stares at the floor. "How much time do I have?" he asks, his voice fragile.

Steinfield props the chart under one arm and shoves his hands into the pockets of his coat. "Four, six weeks at the most without the radiation. If we start treatment now, we might be able to extend that to about six months."

Hamilton Senior clucks his tongue and grunts. "Six months."

"How rough would the radiation be on him?" Bruce asks.

"Pretty damn rough," Steinfield says gravely.

"I don't want any radiation," Hamilton Senior says.

Ham reaches out to his father's shoulder. "But Dad it's the only thing th—"

"No. What's the point?"

"You'd have another Christmas," Christina says. "Holidays with your family."

Ham's father laughs bitterly. "Be too weak to enjoy 'em," he says. He looks at the doctor. "What do you think?"

Steinfield licks his lips. "It's your decision, Mr. Bradford. If you opt to forgo the treatment, legally there's nothing I can do to stop you."

"But do you think it would be worth it?" Hamilton Senior asks.

Steinfield looks at him. "Honestly, no, I do not. If you're more concerned with quality of life than with time, I don't see any reason to go through with radiation. I would opt for hospice instead."

Ham cannot believe what he is hearing. "You're practically letting him kill himself," he tells Steinfield.

Christina grabs his arm. "Ham. . . "

"Well, you are."

Steinfield shakes his head. "I'm simply telling him what his options are, Mr. Bradford. It's strictly his decision about what he wants to do."

Ham is practically shaking with rage. "I don't think my father is in the state of mind to decide that kind of thing right now."

"My state of mind is fine," Hamilton Senior snaps. "I'm not gonna be hooked up to machines for six months and let this hospital bilk me out of my money. I'm not gonna be weak as a cat from radiation treatments. I've seen it happen, son. I don't want that to happen to me."

Ham sighs and looks at Bruce. Bruce is staring at the floor. "I agree with Dad," he tells Ham.

You would, you prick, Ham thinks. He looks back at his father. "So what do you want to do?" he asks him.

"Take me home," Hamilton Senior says. He looks at Steinfield. "You can give me something for the pain, right?"

Steinfield nods. "Yes, sir. I can prescribe some medication. Some shots you can self-administer if that's what you want."

"Take me home," Ham's father says again. "I told you once I didn't want to die here."

"You're not staying at home by yourself," Ham

tells him.

"He's right, there," Steinfield says. "You need someone to stay with you all the time. A nurse perhaps. But hospice can't take care of you twenty-four hours a day."

Hamilton Senior is shaking his head. "I don't want a stranger in my house. Going through my things. Stealing from me."

Christina tugs at Ham's arm. "I've got an idea," she whispers. "Why not move him to your house?"

Ham looks at her. "*My* house?"

"Sure. You've got that spare bedroom."

"My computer's in there," he says. "And my Soloflex. It's my office."

She frowns. "Ham, you can move that computer somewhere else. And when's the last time you used that damned Soloflex?"

"But I can't stay with him," Ham says. "I've got a job. Responsibilities."

"*I* can stay with him," Christina says.

"What about your office? How're you gonna do business?"

She shrugs. "I could do some work out of your house," she says. "And Sandy could take care of the office for me. It really wouldn't be that big of a deal."

Ham blows out a breath. "You sure you want to do this?"

"Yes, honey," she says. "I wouldn't have suggested it otherwise."

Ham looks at his father. "How's it sound to you, Dad?"

His father nods. "Pack my bags."

Ham grunts. "I guess it's all settled, then."

2

Dad is sleeping.

Christina closes her copy of *Redbook* and quietly slips it under her chair, then yawns. She looks at her watch. Two o'clock. It took exactly thirty minutes for Ham and Bruce to move everything out and the medical equipment people to bring in the hospital bed. Ham's father went to sleep almost immediately and has been dozing now for about two hours. Christina is glad; he probably didn't get much rest in the hospital.

So far he has not seemed to be in much pain. She looks at the bottle of pills on the table beside him; guiltily, she wonders if she should hide them. From Kipp.

That's ridiculous, she thinks. Kipp might smoke pot, but she really doesn't know whether or not he's on anything else. She knows Ham talked to him, but she doesn't know what he said. She also doesn't know if it did any good.

She steps lightly from the room and down the hall to Kipp's door. Surprisingly, it is unlocked. She eases it open and peers in. The shades are drawn, and the room is dark. She turns on the light. How can he stand it in here? She looks at the posters that are plastered on his walls, pictures of greasy, tattooed rock stars and anorexic girls in swimsuits. Papers are scattered all over the floor, mostly schoolwork. She picks up a typewritten report. "Herman Melville" by Kipp Bradford. She leafs through it. On the last page is his grade: D+. Beneath it, the teacher has scrawled: *We need to discuss this. Is there a problem? Come see me.*

Christina shivers. *Is there a problem?* She drops the report back on the floor.

Quietly, she opens the top drawer of Kipp's bureau

and rifles through it. Underwear and T-shirts, a ball-point pen with the logo of Ham's bank on it, three CDs, and a savings passbook showing a balance of forty-three dollars. She eases the drawer closed, her hands shaking. Nothing out of the ordinary. The other drawers hold only clothes—concert T-shirts and jeans mostly.

Is there a problem?

Why is she doing this? It's almost as if she is watching a movie, watching someone else snoop through Kipp's room. *I've got to stop this*, she tells herself. She stands straight and catches a glimpse of herself in the mirror—pale face and stringy hair. Like a frantic junky.

Is there a problem?

She slides open the closet door. On the top shelf she finds several ball caps, a rap CD that Ham told Kipp he couldn't buy, an old Mouse Trap game with one corner of the box torn off, a pair of sweat-stained sneakers, a souvenir mug from Epcot full of pennies, and several issues of a porno magazine called *Slick*. With trembling fingers, she leafs through one of the magazines; the pages turn stiffly, caked with crusty, dried semen. Most of the women in the magazine sit with their legs spread wide, holding open their vaginas. Sickened, Christina replaces the magazines and her fingers hit something hard.

It is a knife, a kind of dagger. It has a leather-wrapped handle and ornate carvings in the stainless steel blade depicting an orgy. Biting her lip, she shoves the knife back on the shelf beneath the magazines.

Is there a problem?

She sinks down on Kipp's unmade bed, feeling chill bumps creep across her flesh.

Before she can stop herself, she pulls open the drawer to his bedside table and shuffles through the contents: three more porn magazines, an opened box of condoms, a program from the homecoming dance, a German coin dated 1925, two pencils with broken leads, and a hardcover book with no dustjacket. *Dark Pleasures.* She opens it and thumbs through the pages. Nothing but pictures of naked women being chained, shackled, whipped, and bound. And one photograph of a girl on her hands and knees, wearing nothing but a leather bra. Her bottom is thrust high in the air. Behind her, an obese, hairy man in a leather vest and mirrored sunglasses holds a dagger, its point poised at her anus. In his other hand he grips his erect penis. He is grinning broadly beneath his bushy black beard. The dagger is exactly like the one in Kipp's closet. The book lies open easily here, as if it is turned to this page often.

Christina closes the book, horrified, then shoves it back in the drawer. Her hands are shaking and sweaty. *My God, my God,* she thinks. Why would a sixteen-year-old boy want such a thing?

Heart pounding, she turns out the light and steps back into the hall. Why did she do that? Why did she go through Kipp's things? She didn't find any drugs, which she was afraid of, but in a way she almost wishes she had. Instead of the other. Instead of that book. That horrible picture. That knife.

My God, what is wrong with Kipp? What kind of boy would like that kind of stuff? She shivers and clutches her stomach; she is going to vomit, she knows it.

What will Ham say? Should she tell him? Should she keep it to herself?

She thinks of the teacher's note again: *Is there a problem?*

She sinks onto the sofa, her eyes watering. *Is there a problem? Is there a problem? Is there a problem?*

3

Kipp has been sitting in the boys' restroom for thirty minutes now, waiting until it might be safe to sneak out of school and head home. He really did not feel like sitting in algebra class and looking at that mother-fucking Mills. He really needs a joint, but as sure as he lights one up, the smoke detector in the ceiling will go off.

His ass is numb from sitting on the toilet, but his dick is stiff and pointing straight up. He has been thinking about Amber. Mostly, he has been thinking about slapping the shit out of her, about how his hand would sting at the impact and how her face would turn red with the prints of his fingers. She would probably scream. But that stinging in his palm—that's what he imagines over and over. He slaps his thigh and loses himself in the pleasure of the sound, of the sudden burning on his leg and hand. He hits himself again and again as his other hand squeezes his erection. And suddenly, he is thinking about his knife. His special knife. About plunging it into Amber's ass, into Amber's pussy. Just like in the book. Just like in the picture. And then he is coming, intensely and violently, as the thoughts flash through his mind—the knife, the blood, the slap, the sting of his palm against her soft flesh. . .

Slowly, heart pounding, he opens his eyes and finds himself sitting back on the toilet. Quickly, he pulls off a long sheet of toilet paper and cleans himself up. God, what if somebody had walked in? His thigh is red and stinging where he slapped himself. He pulls up his jeans and steps over to the sink to wash his hands. His face is flushed and sweaty, and perspiration has dripped onto his glasses. He takes them off and wipes the lenses on the tail of his shirt.

Outside, the hall is cool and empty. He passes the droning classes toward the side door to the parking lot. And suddenly he sees Amber. She is sitting in Mrs. Morales's study hall, one strand of auburn hair tossed back over her shoulder, her round eyes focused on the English homework in front of her.

He remembers his fantasy—the knife working its way into her anus.

He motions to her, and she sees him. He stands back and listens as she asks to be excused and her steps come closer to him. She emerges into the hall and stands before him, her arms crossed over her breasts like a shield. "What do you want?" she asks flatly.

"What's going on?" he says.

She rolls her eyes. "I'm in study hall," she says. "I'm working."

He licks his lips. "When are we going out again?"

She laughs bitterly. "Not for a long time." She looks at him. "Did you drag me out here just to ask that?"

"I'm sorry about what happened the last time. I want to make it up to you."

Amber runs her fingers through her hair and stares at the ceiling. "Kipp. . . "

"Please."

She looks at him. "Kipp, I don't want to see you anymore."

He blows out a breath, incredulous. "Why not?"

She is shaking her head. "I just don't think it will work. We're just not right for each other."

He grunts. "So you're fucking somebody else, is that it?"

She turns back toward the class. "Just leave me alone, Kipp."

Rage burns in his gut, and he wishes he had that knife here. He would show her how it was to really be fucked.

"Fine," he croaks.

She turns back to him once more. "Don't call me." Then she is gone.

He watches her go. He is chewing the inside of his mouth. Fine. Who needs the fucking bitch?

* * *

The first thing he sees when he pulls onto his street is Christina's BMW in the drive. Terrific. Just what he needs. He's not sure when he started hating her, but now it's to the point where he can't stand the sight of her. That and listening to her whiny-assed voice.

He knows something is different as soon as he steps into the house. He walks silently through the foyer, toward the hall, toward his room. And when he reaches Ham's office a wave of shock hits him when he sees his grandfather lying there asleep in a bed with clean white sheets. Christina sits in a chair beside the bed, an open magazine in her lap. She looks up and jumps as she sees him. "Kipp," she breathes. "You scared me to death."

"What's Granddad doing here?" he asks.

She puts down the magazine and slips out into the hall, closing the door behind her. He never realized before how short she is; he stands half a head taller than she. She backs up in the doorway, her arms crossed.

Just the way Amber looked when she talked to him.

"Your dad moved him here," she whispers. "He's terminal, Kipp. The cancer's in his bones and his kidneys."

Kipp blows out a breath. "That's too bad," he says.

"Yeah. He's decided not to take any radiation treatments. The doctor said he only has a few weeks left."

"So why bring him here? Why didn't he stay in the hospital?"

"He didn't want to stay there. He wanted to go home, but Ham wouldn't let him. So he moved him here." She blows out a breath and brushes a strand of hair from her eyes. "I'll be staying with him all day. And there'll be hospice nurses in and out."

Kipp looks at her. "So basically he's just here to die."

Christina stares at the floor, nodding. "In a manner of speaking."

"Great," he says sarcastically. He heads down the hall to his room. "Call me when dinner's ready."

When he turns the knob on his door, he knows something is wrong. Fuck! He forgot to lock his room. He steps inside and slams the door behind him. He turns on the light.

Someone has been in here. All the drawers of his bureau are shut tight; he never does that. And his closet door is open; he always keeps it closed. He reaches up and feels through the stack of magazines until he finds the knife. It is underneath them, and he always keeps it beside them.

Someone has been in here, all right. And she was very careless.

4

Bruce knows he used too much cologne. That Polo; he knew he shouldn't have put it on. It's several years old, and it's starting to smell like old cigars. But he didn't want to wear Old Spice. Not on a date.

He pulls up in front of Kelly's apartment and kills the engine. The complex is low-rent but not shabby. He can even see the fence around a tennis court and a hint of a swimming pool hiding under the snow toward one side. Kelly might not make much money clerking at the Gas-N-Pack, but it looks like she knows how to find a bargain.

He blows out a white puff of nervous breath as he tramps toward her door and raps against the frame with his knuckles. Kelly is at the door at once, dressed in a red angora sweater, jeans, and black leather boots. "Come on in," she says.

Her apartment is small but neat and uncluttered. One corner holds a red and yellow crate full of dolls and games. A portrait of Kelly's daughter, an elfin-looking tow-head in a navy-blue dress, is on prominent display on one of the walls. "Where's Amanda?" he asks.

"She's at my mom's," Kelly answers, heading toward the back of the apartment. "Let me get my coat."

"You've got a nice apartment," Bruce says, looking around.

"Thanks." She emerges wearing a leather bomber jacket. "I really lucked out finding this place," she says.

Bruce feels a shudder of embarrassment as Kelly slides into the broken-down Nissan. "Excuse the car," he says. "I've thought some about trying to buy a newer one, but this one's paid for and I hate to spend the money."

"I know what you mean," Kelly says, buckling her seat belt. "I wish mine was." She leans back in her seat. "So where're we going?"

"El Toro de Cancun," Bruce says, pulling out onto the highway.

"I know where that is," Kelly says. "I've never been there but I've heard it's good."

"It is."

"Any idea what the name means?"

Bruce laughs. "'The Bull of Cancun.'"

"Lovely," Kelly says.

* * *

A few minutes later, they are sipping on jumbo margaritas and munching on tortilla chips and salsa. "So how's your dad?" Kelly asks around a bite. "Last time I talked to you he wasn't doing too well."

Bruce nods. "Yeah, we found out today he's terminal."

Kelly frowns. "That's terrible," she says, shaking her head. "I'm sorry to hear that."

"Yeah. The cancer's in his bones and his kidneys now. He probably doesn't have long."

"That's a shame."

Bruce takes a gulp of margarita. "So tell me about your parents. You never say much about them."

"Well, my dad died a few years ago. Heart attack. My mom still lives in our old house. She's retired now. She used to work at the hospital as a nurse's aide. She keeps Amanda for me now while I'm at work or when I'm in school."

Bruce looks up. "School?"

Kelly nods. "Didn't you know? I'm going to the

Health Tech Center. I'm studying medical transcription."

"I didn't know that."

"I should finish up next May."

"That's great."

"Yeah. Then I can quit the Gas-N-Pack and get a real job."

Bruce feels a sting of hurt. That will mean he won't see her anymore. "Maybe you can come back and visit."

She laughs. "I might do that." She takes a bite of a chip. "Did you go to school?"

Bruce nods, swallowing a drink of margarita. "Yeah."

"Where?"

Here it comes, he thinks. "Centre College."

Her eyes widen. "Really? That's a pretty exclusive school. What'd you major in?"

"Economics."

She rolls her eyes. "God, I hate economics. How in the world could you major in that?"

He shrugs, smiling. "I liked it."

She laughs. "Yuck." She stirs her drink with her straw. "So how come you're not in banking or something? Or on Wall Street? Why are you working at the Gas-N-Pack?"

"I didn't finish my degree," he says, staring at the table.

"Oh." She takes another chip and looks away. "Boy, I'm starving," she says.

Bruce watches her, wondering what she is thinking. He wonders if she thinks his not finishing school had anything to do with his being in prison. But she won't ask, he knows; she's much too polite.

He thinks about her wanting to quit the Gas-N-Pack. What does she think about him, a thirty-seven-year-old man stuck there in a dead-end job and no prospects of getting out? Does she just think he's lazy—too shiftless to look for something better? Does she think he's just dizzyingly happy there?

He watches her light a cigarette and study the bullfight mural on the wall above them. And he wonders what she is thinking.

* * *

Bruce's heart is pounding as they pull back into the parking lot of Kelly's apartment complex. After dinner they went dancing at the Lone Star, a country-western bar on the boulevard. It was the first time Bruce had been dancing since college. Now his hips are sore and his feet and legs ache. Holding her close during the slow dances was like embracing a long-lost dream. And the joy that flowered in his chest overflowed to his face and plastered a silly grin on his lips. Not even his first kiss in high school could compare to this feeling.

"Well, thanks," she says. "I had fun."

"Me, too." He clears his throat, trying to keep his voice from quivering.

She looks around. "Do you care to walk me to the door? I feel pretty safe in this neighborhood, but you never know."

He smiles and steps out into the cold. "You think you might want to go out again?" he asks.

She nods. "Sure."

"When?"

She laughs. "I don't know. We'll talk about it."

"Okay."

They step up to her door, and she fumbles in her purse for her keys. "Thanks for dinner," she says, looking at him.

He bends closer, his heart thudding in his ears. Her perfume fills his head, and he is dizzy. "Can—can I kiss you goodnight?" he stammers.

She laughs giddily. "I'd wonder about you if you didn't."

And suddenly he pressing his lips against hers, tasting her, and the warmth spreads through him. The sharp air and the snow are a million miles away.

TEN

1

It is Saturday morning. Ham wakes up slowly, stretching. The room is cold. He shivers and wraps himself in the sheet. He forgot to turn the heat up last night before he went to bed. He wonders if Dad is cold.

He reaches for his heavy robe and steps into his slippers. Through the window he can see the sun shimmering across the last remaining patches of snow in the front yard. He remembers how winter days once were, when Kipp was younger. The uncontainable excitement when the radio announcer gave the school closings for the day. How Kipp would stay outside for hours, building snowmen, sledding, throwing snowballs with his friends. How Ham would have to call him and call him to get him back inside to warm up. How they would sit at the dining room table with steaming hot cocoa or a pizza and stare out at the back yard, at the snow drifting down. The scorched smell of Kipp's wet mittens drying on the heat register in the foyer. Kipp's face red and sweaty and cold, his glasses steaming up when he came inside. The precious few times Ham and Jill played with Kipp in the snow, pulling him on the sled around the back yard.

There are some old home videos of that, he remembers, stored in the closet of his office. Where Dad is now. Where Dad lies dying.

He steps into the hallway, consciously avoiding looking toward Kipp's door, and shuffles down to Dad's room. Peeking inside, he sees his father lying on his side, mouth open, eyes clenched shut, as if in a silent scream. Dad's scrawny arms are bare; Ham pulls the cover up and tucks it around him. He watches for a moment, watches for his father's chest to rise and fall, then steps over to the closet. On the top shelf he finds the video camera and about two dozen digital video cassettes in a cardboard box. He pulls it all down and tip-toes out.

In the den, he runs power and video cables to the camera, then digs through the box of tapes until he finds one marked "Winter 2000." He pops it into the camera and hears it whir to life.

The image of the snow-covered lawn blazes onto the television screen. Jill trudges by, pulling three-year-old Kipp on his red plastic sled. They look toward the camera and wave. "Wave at Daddy," Jill says to Kipp. She is wearing a puffy down coat and a yellow cap; tufts of her blonde hair peek out around her collar. Her face is flushed and vibrant, glowing, and Ham remembers that was around the time they thought she might be pregnant again. Jill picks up a handful of the slushy snow and throws it toward the camera. "Hey, watch it!" Ham hears himself say. Jill giggles and throws some more. Kipp is laughing, pointing with his red mittens. He scoops up more snow and throws with Jill. Then he picks up some and holds it up to his face to taste it. "No," Jill tells him, pulling his hands down. Kipp jerks away. He begins to cry, running toward the camera. Ham zooms in on Jill. She is laughing. She smiles into the camera. Cut to: Jill is in the kitchen, fixing coffee. She turns toward the camera and squints at the bright lights. "Good grief, Ham," she says. Kipp comes running in, holding a page torn from a Bugs Bunny coloring book. He has scribbled purple crayon all over Bugs' face. "Mommy, I colored a picture for you," he says. Jill takes it from him and looks at it, laughing. "That's really good, Sweetie," she tells him. She shows it to the camera. Ham zooms in on the picture, then pans over to Jill's face. She blows him a kiss. The screen turns dark, then solid blue as the tape ends. He swipes a hand over his face and is not surprised when his fingers brush away tears.

There is a knock on the front door. Ham looks at the clock: half-past eight. Must be Christina. He shuffles over to the door, wiping his eyes on the sleeve of his robe. She must have forgotten her key.

But when Ham unlocks the door, he is surprised to see Bruce standing on the front porch. "Bruce," he says stupidly.

Bruce peers inside behind Ham. "Can I come in?"

Ham steps back. "Sure."

"You weren't still in bed, were you?"

"No." He motions toward the television. "Just sitting here watching some old home movies." He heads toward the kitchen. "You want some coffee? I was just about to fix some."

Bruce shakes his head. "No thanks." He follows

Ham through the den to the kitchen. "Dad awake?"

Ham pulls the canister of coffee from the cabinet. "I checked in on him while ago and he was still asleep."

Bruce pulls out a chair and sits down at the kitchen table. "He really looks frail, doesn't he? Like he's so weak he can't even sit up."

Ham nods, pouring water into the coffeemaker. "It seems like he's really going fast. He's lost so much weight the past couple of weeks. And ever since he came home from the hospital he just doesn't have any strength." He sits down across from Bruce. "It's almost like he's given up."

Bruce looks out the window. "I hate seeing him like this. It's scary. You know?"

Ham nods. "Yeah." They sit in silence for a few minutes, listening to the coffee brew. Ham has no idea what to say to Bruce; it's just like it was the other night when he came over for dinner. When you haven't spoken to someone in fifteen years, there is nothing to say. And then, there is much to say. Maybe so much that you don't know where to begin, that you don't know how to form the words. When the coffee pot begins to gurgle, Ham gets up and pulls down a mug. "You sure you don't want some coffee?" he says.

"I'm sure. I'll be going to bed about ten-thirty, and it'll just keep me awake."

Ham looks back at him. "Oh, that's right. You're on third shift."

"Yeah. Have been for quite a while now."

Ham sits back down with his coffee and takes a tentative sip. "So how're things going?"

"All right," Bruce says. He leans back in his chair, his hands behind his head. His worn sweater pulls up, revealing his rotund belly bulging beneath a grungy T-shirt.

Ham still wants to hate Bruce. When he thinks of the misery Bruce caused their parents. When he thinks of Bruce forcing that girl to have sex with him. When he thinks of the embarrassment he caused to the family. When he thinks of how Bruce being his brother probably stunted his career. When he thinks it took Bruce almost ten years to come and see about Dad. When he thinks he has had to care for Dad all this time and Bruce has not lifted a finger to help.

But he looks at Bruce's belly, the stained undershirt and ragged sweater. He looks at Bruce's red, tired eyes. His greasy, receding hair. His pasty complexion. And Ham's revulsion almost gives way to pity. Ham takes a sip of coffee and clears his throat. "Are you doing okay? Financially?"

Bruce blinks. "Yeah. I'm all right."

"You sure?"

"I'm making it."

Ham looks at him. He hears the defensiveness in Bruce's voice, and he almost feels embarrassed to be sitting here in his large house with his antiques and fine things around him. Right now he wishes he was more modest, more capable of living like his father. "If you need anything . . ."

"I'm fine," Bruce says with finality. He looks back toward the outside.

"Ham," Dad calls from his room.

Ham begins to stand, but Bruce motions him down. "I'll go," he says.

"He probably needs some help getting to the bathroom," Ham tells him.

Bruce nods. "I'll help him." He heads out of the kitchen.

Ham sits completely still until he hears Dad greet Bruce, until he hears them shuffling toward the bathroom. Then he relaxes in his chair and takes another sip of coffee.

2

Christina and Sandy are sitting in a booth at the Pizza Inn, just two blocks away from the real estate office. They used to come here for lunch quite often, sharing a large pizza and trying to wolf it down before time to get back to work. But then Sandy began complaining about her weight and how none of her clothes seemed to fit right anymore, and the pizza lunches gave way to turkey sandwiches and grilled chicken salads from the deli across the street. But now when they need a night out together they splurge and head downtown to pig out.

Sandy takes a sip of her Coke. "The crowd's a bit different on Saturday night, isn't it?" she says, looking around. Teenagers on dates and families with little kids fill the restaurant. It is noisy with excited screams from children and the bass thud from the jukebox. "How's Ham's father?" she asks.

Christina shakes her head. "Not too good. I don't think he'll last four weeks. I don't think *I'll* last four weeks. I probably would have stayed there tonight, but Ham just insisted I get out for a while. These past couple of days have been so depressing. Just sitting there. Waiting for him to die."

"Maybe you oughta take some of Ham's happy pills," Sandy jokes.

Christina laughs humorlessly. "I've thought about it, believe me."

Strangely, Ham has been so distant this week. Emotionally and physically. Perhaps he is already grieving. He moves through the house like an automaton, his expression dead and trance-like. She wonders if the anti-depressants are making him sleepy and laconic, or if they are helping by lessening the pain of watching his father languish in his deathbed. If that's the case, maybe they are simply keeping him afloat above the unfathomable darkness of an even deeper depression. All she knows is that she is more and more confused by his behavior. By his inability to feel. By her own inability to understand.

She has avoided Kipp since yesterday afternoon. The image from that book—*Is something wrong?*—swims through her mind with nauseating clarity. That nasty-looking man. The look—of pain? pleasure?—on the girl's face. That knife. The twin to the one she held in her hands.

She thinks again, why would he want something like that? What kind of twisted perversion is coursing through his brain?

That intricate carving on the polished silver blade—long-legged, squatting women with flowing hair; muscle-bound, bearded men with grotesquely exaggerated erections—it was almost like some ancient Roman tableau. Like the ones in the secret rooms at Pompeii where you have to tip the tour guide an extra thousand lira to see them.

But what could possibly be the purpose of such an object? She shudders, thinking of the possibilities.

Sandy is looking at her, concerned. "Are you all

right, Chris?"

"Yeah." She sips at her iced tea. "I'm fine." She smiles as the waitress sets their pizza down on the table and serves them each a slice. The aroma of the pepperoni is heavenly. "I'm starved," she says.

Sandy is pulling gingerly at her slice with her teeth. "Hot!" she announces.

Christina laughs. And that's when she sees Kipp. He is in a booth across the restaurant with Brett Mitchell and two girls. She can't see his face, but she knows it's him. And he is not with Amber. He is hugged up with the girl beside him, and his hand is idly stroking the side of her breast. She watches in sickening fascination as, beneath the table, the girl's hand rubs Kipp's crotch. The two of them are carrying on a nonchalant conversation with Brett and the other girl as if they are all at a church social.

"My God," Sandy says, following Christina's stare. "Isn't that Kipp?"

Christina nods, her mouth open and the slice of pizza still in her hands. The smell of the food is suddenly heavy and greasy, and her stomach tightens with revulsion at the thought of eating. She needs to talk to Ham. Tonight.

3

Kipp stirs drowsily as the gray Sunday morning light creeps into his room around the edge of the blinds. His dick is stiff, straining against his underwear. He reaches down, rubbing the head with his thumb. He is thinking about last night. About that hot bitch he picked up at the mall. About the blowjob she gave him in the back seat of Brett's car. God, nothing has ever felt that good.

Angela is her name. She wrote her phone number on the back of his hand with a red felt-tip pen. He squints to read it in the darkness: 555-1783. His crotch throbs with pleasure at the thought of her. Her long blonde hair, slim legs. Her hot pussy, so wet at the touch of his fingers. He wonders about how it would feel to tickle her cunt with the tip of the knife, exploring all the folds of skin, just before he does her. Just before he shoves the blade in all the way.

His orgasm is swift and explosive, and the semen soaks through the material of his briefs, dripping onto the bed, and he wipes his fingers on the sheet.

He yawns and glances at the clock. Five-thirty. He rolls his eyes, but he knows he is up for the day. Sleep will not come again.

He slides from the sheets and steps out of his wet underwear, wadding them up and pitching them toward his clothes hamper, then pulls up a fresh pair from the basket of clean laundry by the door.

He peeks out the door into the dark hallway. His father's door is still closed. He tip-toes out into the silence, adjusting his glasses, and slips down toward the den.

Granddad's door is open. Kipp stands outside the room and watches the huddled shape of his grandfather on the bed, watches the form rise and fall with each straggling breath. Still alive. When is it going to be over? The stench from the room is starting to creep through the whole house—the smell of Lysol mingled with shit and piss. God, it's making him sick.

He shuffles into the den, to the liquor cabinet in the corner, and pulls out Ham's Wild Turkey. He unscrews the top and takes a drink, waits for the burn to web its way through his stomach, then takes another and replaces the bottle.

He thinks about Angela again. About her hot mouth, her probing tongue. But his dick is too spent to rise again just now. My God, he realizes, he doesn't remember her last name.

He wishes he had a cigarette.

"You're up early," Ham says behind him.

Kipp whirls around at the voice, then straightens up as his father moves toward him in his robe. "Couldn't sleep," he says.

Ham brushes past him on his way to the kitchen. "We need to talk," he says.

Kipp leans against the doorframe. "What about?"

Ham turns toward him. "What's the matter with you, son?"

"What do you mean?"

Ham leans against the counter. "Are you still smoking pot?"

Kipp blows out a breath. "Oh, Dad, not again."

Ham grabs his arm and pulls him up to his face. "Tell me."

Kipp jerks away, glaring at his father. "What's the matter with *you*, Dad?"

"There's nothing wrong with me."

"Bullshit," he says, and he relishes the consternation he sees briefly in Ham's eyes. "Why are you so concerned about me all of a sudden?"

"Because I think something's wrong with you. You never used to act like this. You never used to be so. . . angry all the time. I just think something is bothering you."

Kipp stares at the ceiling above his father's head. "If it's the weed that's bugging you, I'll quit. I swear. I won't touch it again."

"I wish I could believe that."

Kipp looks at him. "You don't believe me?"

"No, I don't."

"Fine." Kipp turns to walk away.

"Did you break up with Amber?"

Kipp looks back at his father. "How did you know that?"

Ham shrugs. "Just a guess. Chris saw you and Brett at the Pizza Inn last night. With those girls."

Rage suddenly boils in Kipp's stomach. "So is she following me now? Spying on me?"

"She wasn't spying, Kipp. She was there with Sandy. They were having dinner." Ham drops his gaze. "She said you and the girl you were with were fondling each other."

Kipp feels his face flush. "So?"

"In public."

Kipp bites his tongue, trying to choke back a laugh. What would his father say if he knew what else happened last night? "Does Christina get her jollies watching other people make out?"

"Stop it," Ham says sharply. "Stop talking about her like that."

"What else did she tell you?" Kipp asks, thinking about her snooping through his room. He would love to take his knife and shove it up that bitch's tight cunt. To hear her scream.

"She didn't tell me anything else," Ham says, but Kipp isn't so sure; something in his father's eyes tells him there is more to the story. Ham clears his throat.

"We'll talk about this later."

"I'm going back to bed."

"Fine."

* * *

At nine-thirty, Christina arrives, stopping by on her way to church. Ham is in the shower when she walks through the front door. Kipp is waiting for her, now wearing a pair of sweat pants with the cuffs pushed up above his calves, sitting on the couch watching *The Real World* and scrolling through Facebook on his phone. "Hello, Christina," he says, not taking his gaze off the screen.

"Hi, Kipp," she says.

He looks at her, and he can almost see a tinge of fear in her eyes. He stares back at the phone. "Dad talked to me this morning," he says. "He said you saw me last night."

She moves toward him. "Kipp, I'm just concerned—"

He leaps off the couch. "Why can't all of you just leave me the hell alone? I can't do anything without everybody in this house knowing about it."

Christina seems on the verge of tears. "I just wondered about you and Amber."

Kipp laughs. "Amber, bullshit. You were just spying on me. Did you follow us all night?"

Christina looks away. "No. I didn't follow you at all."

He wants to say, *Too bad, because you missed seeing me get the blowjob of my life.* But he whispers, "I don't want you to tell Dad anything else about me. You got it?"

Christina nods, and now he can see that she is

really scared. "I won't," she says.

He inches up to her. "And the next time you go snooping through my room, you better have a fucking good reason."

He turns and trudges down the hall, toward his door. He is horny again.

4

Bruce is standing beside the doors to the Gas-N-Pack, drinking decaffeinated coffee and staring out at the dawn breaking over the interstate. Even this early on a Sunday morning, the road is already flowing with traffic.

He looks at his watch and smiles. Seven-thirty. Kelly will be in any time now.

Kelly. God, he knows he is falling in love. The thought of her fills him with warmth as real as the warmth of the cup in his hand. His lips still burn with the memory of her kiss. He can feel his heart pounding, feel excitement building in his arms and legs—all from just thinking about her.

He takes a sip of coffee. When is he going to tell her? What will he say?

"By the way, Kelly," he says aloud to himself, "I was in jail for rape. And while I was in there, I fucked a few guys. Nothing serious. They didn't mean a thing. Now, will you marry me?"

He blows out a breath and watches the window fog up. In some ways he won't allow himself to enjoy this time with her because he knows it is going to end. He knows when she finds out—when he tells her—it will all be over. No more dates. No more goodnight kisses. No more playful talk at work.

He tosses his cup into the trash and steps back behind the counter. Maybe he shouldn't tell her. Maybe she won't ever find out. But could he keep a secret like that? No way. Sooner or later she would ask about it. He knows it.

Her red Escort pulls into the lot and parks beside his Nissan. She steps out of the car, and he watches her walk toward him. His heart leaps, but whether it's from joy or terror he doesn't know.

"Hey," she says, slipping inside. She steps up to the counter and gives him a kiss on the cheek. He stiffens, surprised, then feels his face flush. "Sorry I'm late," she is saying, "but Amanda had mommy-itis this morning." She shakes out her coat and hangs it up. "She was still crying when I left. I always feel terrible when she does that. Sometimes I think she cries on purpose."

Bruce has fixed her coffee—one sugar and one cream, just the way she likes it. "Here," he says, handing it to her. "Have some breakfast."

"Thanks," she says. She takes a sip, then gazes up at him. "How's it going? Been busy?"

He shakes his head and pulls his money drawer from the register. "No. Pretty slow since about two."

"How's your dad?"

"About the same. I went to see him yesterday. He just gets weaker by the day." He doesn't tell her about helping his dad to the bathroom, how he had to clean up the floor and the toilet seat and help him change pajamas after he pissed all over everything before he could get his pants down. About how his father's face was red and ashamed, how his lips quivered with frustration. About how holding him up took no more effort than picking up a bundle of kindling. About how he was asleep again as soon as Bruce got him in the bed. "I just want to rest," his father told him. "I just want to sleep." Then he closed his eyes. He doesn't tell her about how much effort it took to not cry in front of Ham, or how, when he got back into his car and headed home, he was trembling so heavily that he had to pull over in a health club parking lot to let the spell pass. "It's really hard," Bruce says finally. "I hate seeing him this way."

Kelly puts a hand on his shoulder. "I know."

He puts his money in his compartment, grabs his deposit bag and locks the safe. He blows out a breath. "When are we going out again?"

She shrugs, smiling, signing onto the register. "Whenever you ask."

"How about Tuesday? I'm off that night."

"I'm not sure. My aunt is coming in this week for Thanksgiving. My mom may be having a dinner that night. I'll have to let you know for sure."

"Okay."

She looks up. "You could go over there with me. You could meet my mom and Amanda."

"You don't think your mom would mind?"

"Of course not. It would just be the five of us—me, you, Amanda, Mom, and Aunt Ludah Belle."

He gapes at her. "Ludah Belle?"

She shrugs, rolling her eyes. "Family name."

"Well, I'll call you," he says. He stands there awkwardly, thinking of the kiss she gave him when she came in. Should he kiss her goodbye? He looks at her for a heavy, awkward moment. "See ya."

He steps out into the biting cold, shoving his hands

into the pockets of his jeans. No. He shouldn't tell her.
Not yet.

ELEVEN

1

It is Tuesday.

Ham decided to skip lunch today to try to get caught up on all the work that has piled up since Dad became so ill. An open package of crackers and peanut butter lies on one corner of his desk, lost among the piles of papers and loan folders. Ham has been keying loan information into the computer all morning, and now his eyes are dry and burning from staring at the screen for so long. He sits back in his chair, flexing his hands.

Last night, Dad got worse. This time he wet the bed before Ham could get him up on his feet. And then, while Ham and Christina were changing the bedclothes, he fainted in the chair where he was waiting. When he came to, he was moaning with pain. Ham called Dr. Steinfield; Steinfield said to increase the morphine injections. "It's simply a matter of time," he told Ham.

All the while, Kipp remained on the sofa in the den, watching a football game.

Ham has not confronted Kipp with all that Christina has told him. What she said about the scene in the restaurant was bad enough. But then she described what she found in Kipp's room. "I hadn't planned on snooping," she said. "I don't know why I did it. I was scared. Worried."

"It's okay," he told her.

"But that knife," she said. "Where did he get it?"

Ham shrugged. "Probably off the internet. From some S&M company. Probably where he got the book, too. And the magazines."

"How can they sell stuff like that to teenagers?"

"They don't know how old he is," Ham told her. "They were probably just happy to get his money."

"I think you ought to talk to him about it."

"I don't know about that."

"Why not?"

Ham sighed. "Because I've always thought a person's sexuality was a private matter. It's none of our business."

Christina stared at him, a look of shock on her face. "Ham, he's only sixteen, for God's sake. He's your son and he's living under your roof. If he's doing something he shouldn't, it's up to you to stop him."

Ham could feel anger worming its way through his gut. "But technically you shouldn't have been in his room. I'm afraid if he finds out you were snooping around, he'll never trust us again. And the next time, you might find something worse."

Christina blew out a breath. "I'm just. . . scared." She looked at him. "He scares me, Ham. He's just not the same person he used to be." He realized then that she was crying. "I remember this happy boy who used to stand beside me in church and sing hymns, and his voice was so sweet. And how he used to go places with us—out to dinner or something. Remember that?"

"Yeah."

"And now I see him and it's like, 'My God, who are you?' He's so. . . so angry all the time. And he looks at me and his eyes are just so cold. It's like he's just. . . dead inside."

He thinks about that, and he remembers an old movie he saw once late at night. *The Village of the Damned*, where all the children were strange and emotionless. He shivers. He knows something is wrong with Kipp; he can see it, too. And he can feel Kipp slipping away from him like an old memory his mind just can't quite grab onto.

Kay's voice on the intercom suddenly cuts into the silence. "Ham, Christina's on line three."

He picks up the phone. "Hi, babe."

"Ham, something's wrong," she says frantically.

"What's the matter?"

"I went in to check on Dad and he won't respond. I called Dr. Steinfield and he says he may have slipped into a coma. He told me to call an ambulance."

Ham feels his body going numb. "Have you done that?"

"Yes. They're on their way."

"All right. I'll meet you at the hospital."

He hangs up the phone and stares at it. His heart is thudding sickeningly against his ribcage. He needs to call Bruce.

2

The three of them—Christina, Ham, and Bruce— are sitting in a closet-like waiting room off the emergency lobby. Christina is nauseated—like she will vomit at any time. She knows this is the room where they take you when somebody dies. "The Crying Room," she once heard someone refer to it. A place where families can scream and moan and not disturb the others waiting outside.

Ham has loosened his tie and thrown his jacket over the back of a chair. His legs splayed wide, he sits slumped in the green vinyl chair as if completely drained. His face is white, almost as white as his shirt. My God, he looks old, Christina thinks. New lines seemed to have formed around his eyes overnight, and she almost thinks she can see a few new streaks of gray in his hair.

Bruce is stretched out on a sofa, one foot on the floor, bouncing his leg up and down, up and down. He chews his thumbnail like an old dog nipping at a flea. His black hair sticks out stiffly, comically; he had been in bed only an hour when Ham called him.

Christina crosses her legs and pretends to smooth out the wrinkles in her slacks. The past few days have been so horrible. First Dad. Then meeting Bruce. Then all the mess with Kipp. She feels as though she is in shock—like a victim of some natural disaster. This week seems to have lasted a month—and yet, the days have passed quickly. She has done little work since she has been staying at Ham's; in fact, she has not spoken with a client or shown a house since Dad moved in.

She has not talked to Ham about Kipp since Sunday. Since Kipp threatened her. Actually, he didn't exactly threaten her. It was more of a warning. But his eyes. That hate. She still cringes when she thinks of it. And he knew—somehow—that she had been in his room. And that embarrasses her. But the thought of him, of him with that knife, will not let go. And she wonders, would he use it on her? And if so, how?

She suddenly realizes that she is more afraid now of Kipp than of Bruce. Bruce, who raped a girl fifteen years ago and is now walking around on the streets. Bruce, whom, just a week or so ago, Christina was so afraid of that she was terrified of the possibility of having to spend just a few moments alone with him.

She looks at him now. He's kind of pitiful, really, she thinks. Overweight and balding, not attractive at all. And she remembers the shock of first meeting him, how the juxtaposition of him and Ham side by side was like Danny Devito and Arnold Schwarzenegger in that old movie *Twins*. There is nothing scary about Bruce at all when she thinks about it. He's so soft-spoken. And polite. She remembers how he thanked her for dinner and complimented her. And his flattery wasn't like that of a hormone-driven egotist bent on wooing a woman into bed like so many guys she had seen in bars. He was genuine. He was real. And she knows that she was cold and distant, that she kept her guard up the entire evening. That she was not good at hiding her fear. And she thinks of how glad she was that Kipp was there, how she was depending on Kipp to protect her if Bruce had tried anything. It's almost funny now, she thinks.

Her mind plays over and over that scene in Kipp's bedroom when she pulled that knife down from beneath that stack of semen-encrusted magazines. Thumbing through the pages of that book. A black, hard-cover volume with gold script lettering: *Dark Pleasures*. Shoving everything back into place and stumbling mindlessly down the hall. Bending over the bathroom sink, nearly blind with nausea, scrubbing at her hands with soap and hot water until they were red and numb.

Is there a problem? Oh, yes, she thinks.

She wonders about that English paper with its bold red D+. She wishes she had read it. She wishes she knew how badly Kipp could have written to deserve that grade. Maybe Ham should talk to Kipp's English teacher; she can never remember Kipp ever making lower than a B on anything. But Ham has been so preoccupied lately that he's hardly had time to notice Kipp. At least, that's the way it seems.

She looks up as Dr. Steinfield steps into the room and softly closes the door behind him. He nods at them, then sits on the coffee table facing Ham and Bruce. "Mr. Bradford has passed away," he says.

Christina feels the tears spilling down her cheeks, and her mind races through the morning—finding Dad limp in his bed, trying to rouse him, tearing through Ham's address book to find the doctor's number, the dizzying ride through town in the ambulance. . . All of it a blur.

"He apparently had a mild stroke and slipped into a coma," the doctor is saying, "but he was so weak that his body just wasn't able to hold on. His heart had stopped when he came in, and we tried CPR, but he wouldn't respond."

Ham is staring at the floor. "This is the way he wanted it," he says.

"I'm sorry," Dr. Steinfield says.

Ham nods. "I know you did everything you could." He looks at Christina and squeezes her hand.

3

"My grandfather died today," Kipp says as Brett steps into Kipp's car.

"Sorry to hear that," Brett tells him.

Kipp shrugs. "He was old." He shifts into first and pops off the clutch, squealing his tires down Brett's street. Beside him, Brett is fumbling for his seatbelt. Kipp smiles. What a pussy.

"What was wrong with him again? Cancer?"

"Yeah." Kipp pulls out onto the highway, turning up the Foo Fighters CD as he accelerates. "I'm glad he's dead," he says, and he can feel Brett staring at him. "I've been sick as a dog since Dad moved him in there. He stank. There was no way to get away from that smell. It just made me want to puke every time I walked by there."

"He seemed to go pretty fast," Brett comments quietly. "He must've been really sick."

"Yeah." He looks at Brett. "Didn't take long, did it?"

Brett reaches into the pocket of his coat and pulls out a can of Budweiser. "Wanna beer?"

"Yeah." Kipp holds out his hand and grabs the can, braces it between his knees as he pulls the tab. "Thanks."

He smoked two joints before he picked up Brett, and now his head is thick and fuzzy. Groggy. He takes a sip of beer and feels the cold trickle down his throat. He hadn't realized how thirsty he was.

"Where we headed?" Brett asks.

"The mall." Last night he tried to call Angela, but when he dialed the number she gave him, the woman who answered didn't know her. "Well," he said to her, "would you like to suck my cock?" The woman gasped and hung up. Tonight, though, he is going to look for Angela. He wants to know why she gave him a fake number.

* * *

They have been cruising around the mall now for about an hour, and there is no sign of Angela or her friend Misty. No sign of Misty's teal Corolla. What bitches. If he ever sees Angela again, he just might have to teach her some manners.

"I can't believe she didn't give you her real number," Brett is saying. "You two were getting along great."

"Yeah."

"I mean, she sucked you, man. That Misty would hardly let me feel her tits. And there you were getting sucked off in the back seat."

"Yeah." He wishes Brett would just shut up. He is really getting on Kipp's nerves. He pulls out of the mall lot and heads back toward downtown. "Let's go somewhere else," he says.

Brett is staring out the passenger window. "Have you talked to Amber lately?"

Kipp snorts. "No. Not since she kissed me off." What a bitch. He still burns when he thinks of talking to her in the hallway the other day. *Don't call me.* Man, would he like to do her. Her and Angela at the same time. Amber and Angela locked pussy-to-pussy, rubbing their tits together. Kipp with his knife, probing first Amber's ass, then Angela's. Then shoving the blade in all the way and tearing through Amber's ass to her pussy, then on through to Angela's pussy and slicing through her ass. And the screams. All that blood. Mixing with his come.

"Watch it, Kipp," Brett says. "There's a dog up

there in the road."

And then Kipp sees it: a mangy-looking stray, skinny, its coat matted with mud and dirt. He aims the car at it. Watches its empty eyes staring dumbly into the headlights.

"Look out!" Brett cries.

Kipp speeds up and the dog disappears beneath the hood of the Mazda with the thump and crunch of brittle bones.

"You hit it, Kipp," Brett says stupidly. "You aimed right for it." He is staring at Kipp, his mouth open. "Why did you do that?"

Kipp glances in the rear-view mirror, but the dog is already far behind. "It didn't yelp or anything," Kipp says, taking a sip of beer.

4

Bruce sits on the couch, staring at Brian Williams on the television. Brian's face is green. In fact, the whole picture is green and distorted, as it has been for a couple of weeks now. Like his Nissan, the TV was Bruce's in college, and now it is just about to die. Just like his father.

He almost cannot conceive how quickly Dad went. It was only last Friday that he and Ham moved him into Ham's house. And now it is Tuesday and he is dead. Things have changed so fast.

He reaches for his phone and punches in Kelly's number. Strange how he already has it memorized. When she answers, Bruce feels that warmth spread through him like fine brandy. "Hi," he says.

"Hey." Her voice is light and girlish. "Are we still on for tonight?"

"Well, that's why I'm calling. My dad died this

afternoon."

"Oh, I'm sorry."

"Yeah. So I don't think I'd be much fun."

"That's all right," she says. "Is there anything I can do for you?"

"Nah."

She sighs. "I really hate that. He went pretty fast, didn't he?"

"Yeah. The doctor said he probably had a stroke and went into a coma."

"I just can't get over how quick it all happened."

"Well, from what Ham said, he'd been sick for quite a while, but he wouldn't go to the doctor until just a couple of weeks ago."

Kelly clucks her tongue. "When's the funeral?"

"Thursday at two."

"That's Thanksgiving day," she says.

"Yeah."

"I want to come."

"You don't have to do that," he tells her. "You need to spend that day with your family."

"I want to," she says. "I want to be there with you."

"Are you sure?"

"Yeah. I'm sure."

"But you never even met him."

"Bruce," she says insistently, "I want to go."

Bruce smiles. "All right. I'll talk to you more about it tomorrow."

After he hangs up the phone, he lies back down on the couch, staring again at the green television. She wants to be there, she said. With him. What in God's name is he going to do? He is getting in deeper and deeper with her. She is going to be hurt when she finds out about him. And she will probably not want to see him again. And then he will feel worse than ever before. Why did he ever ask her out? Why did he ever let himself get carried away like that?

Because he was lonely, goddammit. He has lived by himself in this ratty trailer now for eight years. And in all that time he has never had a relationship with anyone. He thinks of that night two weeks ago with Gary, and he cringes with embarrassment. He just needed someone to hold. Someone to hold him back.

And now he might just have that with Kelly. And nothing in the world compares to that feeling of being needed, of the connection between two people. And the thought that it might all end when he tells her terrifies him. And then where will he be?

He is startled by a scratching at the door. He sits up, listening, then steps over the pile of papers and magazines to turn the sound down on the television. He hears it again, faint but persistent.

He creeps to the door and peers out through the blinds, but all he can see is the empty stoop and the last vestiges of snow melting in the muddy yard. The scratching comes again from near the bottom of the door. He slides the chain into place and eases the door open. In the faint light from the television, he sees the two eyes glowing back at him, then an inquiring meow. "Hi, kitty," he says.

He unchains the door and the cat bolts inside behind the chair. Bruce steps around to peer at it where it crouches in the corner. "Come on out, kitty," he whispers. "Come on. I won't hurt you." He holds out his fingers. The cat sniffs at them cautiously.

Bruce moves to the kitchen and pulls a can of tuna from the cabinet. "Kitty, kitty, kitty," he calls in a falsetto voice. At the sound of the can opener, the cat approaches slowly, rubbing against a kitchen chair. Bruce forks the tuna out into a bowl and sets it down on the floor. The cat trots over to it, purring, eating greedily. In a few minutes, the bowl has been licked clean. The cat licks its mouth and settles down to bathe. Bruce bends down and strokes its back, and it arches to his touch. It turns and rubs against his leg.

Bruce grabs a beer from the refrigerator and sinks back onto the couch. He supposes he needs to give the cat a name. He sips on his beer and thinks. A black cat with one white ear; it looks like someone spilled paint on its head. Maybe he should call it Sherwin-Williams. He laughs to himself, staring at the green TV.

He jumps as the cat leaps into his lap. It turns around and lies down, staring up at him.

"Hi, Sherwin," Bruce says.

The cat looks at him, blinking.

TWELVE

1

Ham glances at his watch. Almost two-thirty. Dad's pastor has been rambling now for quite some time. He is an older man, not quite Dad's age, but short and wrinkled and white-bearded. He looks like a Jew, Ham thinks. A rabbi. All he needs is a yarmulke. But he's only a plain Presbyterian minister.

Bruce's girlfriend came to the funeral. Ham is surprised at how attractive she is. And he wonders again: what kind of woman is she to be interested in Bruce? He wonders if she knows how wealthy their father was, if maybe she has her eyes on the Bradford money. And if she does know, he wonders how she found out. Did Bruce tell her? Certainly one look at Bruce should make her question the fact that he is a millionaire's son. Today he is dressed in a navy polyester suit, a short-sleeve blue shirt, and a tie so skinny that it must have been in Bruce's closet since 1983. Not the attire of a wealthy man. So if she knows, Bruce had to tell her. Ham can picture them huddled somewhere in a filthy dive, Bruce describing his inheritance and Kelly taking it all in, wide-eyed, planning and conniving. But maybe he's being too harsh. Maybe she really does care for Bruce. Maybe they really are in love. He noticed how they stood arm-in-arm before the casket last night, how close they sat. How they looked at each other when they thought no one was watching. So if she is only after the money, she's a damned good actress.

Beside him, Kipp sighs. Ham glances at him. His eyes are shut, and Ham wonders what is going on behind the closed lids. He's hardly spoken to Ham or Christina since last week. He probably knows that Chris went through his room.

He scares me, Ham.

Ham shifts his gaze back to the pastor. Kipp has some problems, no doubt. But what teenager doesn't? Kipp isn't the only boy in his class that smokes grass— Ham's certain of it. Hell, Ham himself smoked his share of it in college; everybody he knew did. And he doesn't recall seeing anyone else act this way. Something else is wrong.

Maybe breaking up with Amber has been hard on him. He knows that Kipp was with Amber longer than he dated anyone else. He also knows that they had several fights and stopped seeing each other a few times. And none of those times was like this.

He scares me, Ham.

Maybe Chris has good reason to be afraid. She's right about Kipp changing. Watching those home videos the other day was jarring. At the time, he was so caught up in looking at Jill that he didn't notice. But now he realizes how happy Kipp was back then. How alive he seemed.

And now, seated beside Ham at the funeral, he is lethargic. Cold. More dead than Ham's father in the casket just a few feet away. What is wrong with the boy? He'd like to just take hold of him and shake him. Slap him. Wake him up.

Before him, surrounded by roses and mums, the minister drones on and on. Interminable.

2

Christina squeezes Ham's hand tightly as they step outside to the black limousine. Her other hand clutches a wadded tissue that she has folded so many times it is almost shredded. She didn't cry. She knew she wouldn't. But her mother had taught her that a lady must always carry a handkerchief to a funeral. And since Christina doesn't own a handkerchief, a tissue had to suffice.

She was overwhelmed by the flowers. So many. Most from people she had never heard of—past business associates of Dad's more than likely. The bank sent a gorgeous arrangement of mums—rust and yellow and burgundy. And Sandy sent a potted philodendron with a card that read "For Christina."

Bruce and Kelly slide into the seat opposite them. Kelly is quite pretty in a simple black dress and leather pumps; her hair cascades about her shoulders, soft and loose. Christina can tell by looking at them together that they are in the early stages of romance. She sees it in the way they touch—gently, tentatively. They are still learning each other.

She wonders how long it will be before they behave like she and Ham. She remembers how at first everything with Ham seemed new and exciting. How just a kiss could last a whole evening. How just a touch of Ham's fingertips could make her shiver, blush. And now there is not much kissing. Not passionate kissing anyway. And touching Ham's body has almost become like touching her own. But the love is still there, slowly burning. Glowing. And the hottest kisses she ever had can't compare to that.

Beside her, Kipp sits pressed against the door as if he is recoiling from her. He has not said a word to her all day. She is almost to the point where she doesn't care anymore. She will have to reach that point because she can't take being terrified and anxious twenty-four hours a day. There comes a time when you have to be objective and apathetic. That's the only way you can cope.

"You mind if I smoke?" Kelly asks, and when no one objects, she pulls a cigarette from her purse and lights it with a match from a book with the logo of Ham's bank on it.

"Ham works there," Christina says, motioning to the box. "First State."

Kelly glances at the box as she drops it in her bag. "Yeah, that's what Bruce said. I've banked there for years." She smiles at Ham and cracks her window, blowing smoke at it. "You're in loans, aren't you?" she says to Ham.

"That's right." Ham is smiling politely, but Christina can see the weariness around his eyes.

"I knew I'd seen you there. When I got my car. Roger Carroll was who I talked to."

"Roger's a good guy," Ham says, watching out the side window. Christina looks at the ceiling. She knows that Ham and Roger have barely been civil to each other for about a year now. As Roger's boss, Ham has had several closed-door discussions with Roger about his improper loan documentation, something Ham said could cost the bank thousands of dollars in fines if discovered by the FDIC.

The limo creeps down the highway toward the cemetery, heading the procession. On the opposite side of the road, cars and trucks pull off to the side to let the line of automobiles pass. Christina wonders who started this odd tradition. Granted, it is a sign of stoic Southern respect for the dead, but it still seems macabre. Just like going to the cemetery, she thinks. Only here do people have a funeral and then load everything up and move it for a graveside service. One or the other should be plenty for anyone.

The limo stops, and all of them climb out and file toward the gravesite, where a hideous green tent has been erected to shade the coffin from the sun. Behind the tent, a green tarp covers the mound of dirt that will be used to fill in the grave.

Behind her, Christina hears Kipp mutter, "Jesus, I'll be glad when this is over," and she feels anger ignite in her stomach. A month ago she would have turned and looked at him sharply. A month ago, she might have even told him to be quiet. A month ago, Ham might not have pretended he didn't hear.

She grips Ham's arm tighter as they trudge up the hillside to the grave.

3

Thank God it's over, Kipp thinks, heading into his room and stripping off his tie. The others are in the kitchen, heaping their plates full of the food neighbors have brought by. But he can't stomach the thought of that. Funeral food. Jesus Christ.

He locks the door and drops the tie to the floor, then his jacket. He sits on the edge of the bed and unties his shoes. Adds them to the pile. God it feels good to get out of his clothes. The suit is almost too small for him; when he unbuckles his pants, the skin around his stomach is red-marked and itchy from being squeezed with the waistband. But now he is just in his briefs, and he is cool and comfortable.

The base of his basketball lamp is hollow; inside it he has stored a Zip-Loc bag filled with weed and a few ready-made joints. He pulls out his lighter and a joint and steps over to crack his window just enough so the smoke will go outside.

What a fucking day, he thinks. He drops a CD into the player, and his penis stirs as the speakers thunder with bass. But he's too bummed out to jack off today. He lies down on the bed, taking a drag off the joint. He blows out a stream of smoke, studying the textured plaster on his ceiling; there is a crack that looks like a rabbit. Kipp has named it "Bugs." Bugs has seen all kinds of shit in here; it's a good thing he can't talk.

This has been some holiday. Going to a fucking funeral. They're supposed to be eating turkey and watching football. It's Thanksgiving Day for chrissakes. He picks up his phone and sends a text to Brett: *Where u at?*

Grandmas, Brett replies. *U?*

Home from funeral.

There is a long silence, then the phone buzzes again. *How was it?*

Kipp looks at the question for an eternity, trying to decide what to answer. Finally he taps in a response: *Sucked.* He takes a drag off the joint, then types: *Want to hang?*

Cant today. Family shit. Maybe tomorrow. I'll text you.

Kipp tosses his phone back on the bed. Thank God Ham is not as goofy as Brett's dad. Ham plays golf with Russ Mitchell sometimes, and he usually comes back with a story about some stupid shit Russ pulled on the course. Ham thinks Russ is funny; Brett thinks he's a psycho. Brett says that in the summer Russ will sit out on the lawn in just a pair of swimming trunks, his round belly ballooning over his fat legs, drinking a beer and watching ants. He watches them for hours, fascinated. One Christmas he gave Brett an ant farm. He'd had one as a boy, he said, and now he thought Brett could enjoy watching the ants build a city in the dirt between the two sheets of Plexiglas. A week later, Brett and Kipp took the farm outside and flooded it with the garden hose, mesmerized by the frantic scrambling of the drowning ants. Then they had poured the whole mess out into the yard and hidden the empty farm in the trash. Brett told Russ he had given the ants to Kipp, and Russ believed him. The next time Kipp went over, Russ gave him a book about ants. What a freak.

There is a knock on the bedroom door. Kipp sits up, startled. "What?"

"Kipp?" Ham's voice calls.

"What!"

"Don't you want something to eat?"

"No."

"You sure? There's lots of food in here."

"I'm not hungry."

"There's barbecue. And potato salad."

Jesus, Kipp thinks, rolling his eyes; Ham can be so dense sometimes. "I'm not hungry," he says again.

"I'll eat later."

"All right."

Kipp lies back down.

"Kipp?"

"What is it now?"

"Are you burning something in there?"

Kipp slides onto the edge of the bed. Oh, fuck. "No," he says. "Why?"

"Seems like I can smell something."

Shit. "I don't smell anything."

"Must be the barbecue," Ham says, and Kipp hears him move away from the door.

Kipp lies back down, blowing out a breath. He looks at the crack in the ceiling. "Bugs," he says, "this has just been one fuck of a day."

4

"It was a nice service," Kelly says. She is driving down Ham's street, heading for the other side of town to her apartment, where Bruce's car is parked.

"I thought so," Bruce says. "I'm glad you went with me."

She smiles at him. "Sure."

This afternoon at Ham's went well. The four of them sat and talked liked old friends. Even Christina seemed warmer today, friendlier. In fact, the afternoon went so well that when Bruce looked at his watch, he was surprised to see that it was almost eight o'clock, and night had fallen outside.

Kelly stops at a red light. "Do you want to go to Mom's with me to pick up Amanda? Mom hasn't met you yet, and neither's Amanda. They've both heard a lot about you."

Bruce looks at her. "They have?"

Kelly's face flushes. "Well, yeah. I guess I talk more than I should."

Bruce smiles and looks out the window, watching the passing lights.

* * *

Kelly's mother is slim and handsome, her short, dark hair highlighted with streaks of silver. She greets Bruce warmly. "I'm glad Kelly finally brought you over here," she says. "I was beginning to think you didn't exist."

"Mommy!" Amanda rushes in, her long blonde hair billowing behind her. Kelly sweeps her up and squeezes her. "I missed you," Amanda tells her. She eyes Bruce, then gives him a tight-lipped smile.

"This is Bruce," Kelly says. "Remember? I've told you about him."

"Oh, yeah," Amanda says. She leans toward him. "Are you gonna marry Mommy?"

"Amanda!" Kelly says sharply, and Bruce laughs. Kelly looks at him, red-faced. "I never said that. I swear."

"It's all right."

Amanda is giggling. She turns toward Kelly's mother and holds out her arms to hug her. "'Bye, Nana."

Kelly's mom plants a kiss on her forehead. "'Bye, honey." She looks up at Bruce. "Nice meeting you."

He nods. "You, too."

* * *

"Mom liked you," Kelly says as they pull into the parking lot of her apartment.

"You think so?"

"Yeah."

"I like you," Amanda calls from the back seat.

Bruce turns and smiles at her. "Thank you."

"'Welcome."

Kelly parks the car, and Bruce helps her unload Amanda and the bag of toys Amanda has brought home from her grandmother's. He carries the bag to the door step and sets it down, then digs his keys out of his pocket. "Well, thanks for going," he says again. "I guess I'll head on home now."

She looks at him, her key poised in the lock. "You have to work tonight?"

He shakes his head. "Nah. I'm taking a week off. Ham and I have to wrap up some of Dad's business."

"Why don't you come in for a while?" she asks.

"Well. . ."

Amanda is jumping up and down. "Mommy, it's cold!"

Bruce laughs. "All right. For a little while."

Kelly turns on the lights and follows them inside. "I'll start some coffee," she says.

Bruce shivers. "That sounds good."

"Look what I got, Bruce!" Amanda says. She is holding up a Bedtime Barbie. "Wanna hold her?"

"Okay." He takes the doll and cradles it like a baby. "What's her name?"

Amanda looks at him indignantly. "It's Bedtime Barbie."

"Oh."

She shushes him. "She's asleep," she whispers.

Bruce takes a seat on the sofa, still holding Bedtime Barbie, and glances up at a portrait of Kelly and Amanda. "That's a good picture," he says as Kelly comes in from the kitchen.

"Thanks," she says. "I just picked that up Monday."

Amanda is down on the floor, looking at a row of DVDs. "Mom, can I watch a movie?"

Kelly looks at her watch. "No, honey, it's bedtime."

"But I wanted to watch Snow White."

"Not tonight. It's too late. You can see it tomorrow."

"Can I take it to Nana's?"

"Yeah, that sounds like a good idea."

"Okay."

"Ready for bed?"

Amanda looks at Bruce. "Can I have Bedtime Barbie back?"

He hands it to her. "You don't think she'd want to stay with me?"

"She's sleepy."

"Oh, all right."

Amanda leans over and whispers something in Kelly's ear. Kelly smiles and looks at Bruce. "She wants you to carry her up to bed," she says.

Bruce laughs. "All right."

He picks up Amanda and follows Kelly toward the stairs. "Like a baby," Amanda says, and Bruce turns her over, cuddling her in his arms.

Amanda's room is neat and tidy. "She doesn't play up here much," Kelly explains. "If I'm downstairs, I like her to be down there with me. I have this horror of her falling down the steps and breaking her neck."

Bruce stands in the doorway while Kelly helps Amanda into her gown. Amanda's walls are plastered with posters of Disney characters—Cinderella, Pinocchio, Dumbo. Pictures he remembers seeing as a child. It gives him some comfort. It's good to know that some things never change.

"I wanna kiss Bruce goodnight," Amanda says as Kelly pulls up her covers.

Kelly looks questioningly at Bruce, and he steps over to accept the tickly, sloppy kiss. "Goodnight," he says.

"'Night."

"Coffee's probably ready," Kelly says. "Why don't you go on down and fix us some?"

"Okay."

"Cups are in the dish-drainer."

He heads downstairs into Kelly's bright yellow kitchen and pulls out two stoneware mugs. He has met the family. He is starting to become relaxed with her. And yet, he is afraid. He knows it will end. He knows when she finds out, there will be no more nights like this.

She steps in behind him. "I hope that didn't make you uncomfortable," she says.

"What?"

"Amanda kissing you goodnight."

He hands her the coffee. "Well, I wasn't expecting it, but it didn't make me uncomfortable."

Kelly takes a sip of coffee. "She likes men. She likes to flirt."

Bruce laughs. "I think it's cute."

"It's cute now, but it won't be in ten years." She blows out a breath. "Let's go in the living room."

Kelly sinks back into the couch and lights a cigarette. "I've got to quit smoking," she says. "I know it's not good for me. Or Amanda."

Bruce blows at his coffee, then takes a swallow. "Maybe you just need some encouragement."

She rolls her eyes. "That would be good for a change. Encouragement's something I never got from

Dave. I don't think he believed in it."

"Who's Dave?"

"My ex."

"Oh."

"We were married for three years. It was awful. The whole time I kept thinking, 'Why am I married to this man?' I was just about to leave him when I got pregnant."

"How long have you been divorced?"

"Two years." She laughs. "Best two years of my life."

"Does he ever call? About Amanda, I mean."

She shakes her head and takes a drag of her cigarette. "Bastard hasn't seen her since we split up. He just mails me his little check every month. Doesn't call, come by or nothing."

"That's bad."

Kelly shrugs. "I don't know. I'd just as soon not see him."

"Where does he live?"

"Here in town."

Bruce grunts and takes a sip of his coffee. What kind of a man could just leave someone like Kelly? What would make a man turn his back on a loving wife and a child and walk away from them? Someone who obviously didn't know what he had. Someone who had never lain sleepless in his bed, feverish and hopeless with the idea of spending the rest of his life alone. Someone who was never so achingly desperate that the sweat of his frustration ran ice-cold.

He reaches out for Kelly's hand, and her fingers intertwine with his. And suddenly his lips are brushing hers, and he can feel the softness of her cheek against his face. And his fingertips trace the outline of her breast. And his tongue can taste the coffee and the sweetness of sugar, the bitter tang of her cigarette. The warmth between her legs grows hotter, and his erection is straining to break free. And then she is pulling at his shirt, and he slips it off over his head. He can't meet her eyes; he can feel her gaze boring into his fat stomach. But then she is running her fingers over his smooth chest and exploring his nipples with her tongue, and his belly is forgotten.

* * *

Bruce lies awake in the warmth of Kelly's bed, his hands behind his head, staring up into the darkness. Beside him, Kelly stirs in her sleep, then begins snoring lightly.

He cannot believe he has done this. He has made love to her without telling her about Pamela. He never thought he could let things get so out of control.

Part of him says it's all right. After all, he knows inside that he never committed rape, that Pamela's story was pure fiction.

But what he knows and what he feels cannot change what actually is. He still spent seven years in prison. And he is and always will be labeled a convicted rapist. And that is something that Kelly, even with all her warmth and trust, will not be able to ignore. But he will have to tell her anyway. No matter how much it hurts.

He rolls over onto his side, his heart pounding, his stomach churning. Tonight, he knows, sleep will not come for a very long time.

THIRTEEN

1

Ham sits at his father's kitchen table, an untouched cup of black coffee in front of him. How odd it feels to be here in this house alone. Earlier he turned on the radio that sits on a shelf above the stove, but that started getting on his nerves and he snapped it off. He found a granola bar in the kitchen cabinets, and he ate that and a piece of cheese, and then he found a small box of raisins and he ate those as well. Now he feels sick.

Bruce is coming over this morning to help him search for Dad's insurance policy. He is looking forward to it in a way. Yesterday after the funeral, when the four of them sat at Ham's dining room table and ate and talked, Ham almost felt close to Bruce. The whole evening was like a dinner party. He had almost been tempted to bring out the cards for a round of bridge.

Strange, he thinks, that two brothers could be so different and come from the same parents. Strange, also, that so many years have passed without so much as a phone call, and now they can sit at the same table like the best of friends. Strange that he found nothing strange in that last night.

But he supposes that his thoughts last night were occupied with Kipp. Kipp, who never came out of his room after three o'clock. Ham knows he was smoking pot last night. He could smell it. The scent emanating from around Kipp's door might as well have been a blinking neon sign. The fact that he was doing it doesn't make Ham nearly as angry as the fact that Kipp lied about it. *No, Dad, I don't smell anything.*

This morning he moved all his medications from the bathroom and hid them in his underwear drawer. Why, he's not sure, and he felt guilty the whole time he was doing it, as if he were committing some secret sin. But he just doesn't trust the boy anymore, and he is ashamed for feeling that way. But he is also angry that Kipp has backed him into a corner, and now Ham has no choice but to fight his way out.

He wonders if maybe he should call Ray. Ray could at least give him a professional opinion about the situation. He could tell him whether he thinks Kipp might need some help.

Ham traces his fingertip around the rim of the coffee cup. He already knows the answer to that one. Kipp is in trouble. Something will have to change. People don't do drugs without it catching up to them sooner or later.

But he keeps thinking about Christina. The fear in her eyes. Her lurid description of that book. And he knows she is right: normal sixteen-year-old boys don't get off on sado-masochism. Normal sixteen-year-old boys don't keep orgy daggers in their closets. Normal sixteen-year-old boys don't make their parents afraid to find out more about them.

Ham jumps as he looks up to see the outline of someone standing at the back door, but it is only Bruce. He knocks. "Come on in," Ham calls.

Bruce peeks in around the door. "You home?"

"Hey," Ham says. And suddenly, he feels grateful for Bruce's presence. Grateful for someone to be with him. Grateful for something to take his mind off of Kipp. "Want some coffee?"

Bruce nods. "Sounds good. I can't seem to get going today."

Ham pulls a clean mug down from the cabinet and pours it full. "Rough night?"

Bruce smiles, his cheeks turning bright red. "A late one." He pulls off his Miami Dolphins cap, scratches his scalp through his receding hair, then places the cap back on his head.

"Dolphins, huh?" Ham says, handing him the coffee.

"Yeah." Bruce looks around. "Cream and sugar?"

"Cabinet up there." Ham leans back against the counter. "I saw them play once."

"Really? Got a spoon?"

Ham pulls one out of the drawer behind him. "I was in Washington for an American Bankers conference. Saw 'em play the Redskins."

"Hm," Bruce says, taking a sip of coffee.

"Don't get so excited," Ham says sarcastically.

Bruce looks at him and smiles. "I'm sorry. I don't ever watch much football. I just got this cap free at the store."

"Oh." Ham sits down at the table.

Bruce follows, looking around. "Kitchen hasn't changed much."

"Nothing's changed much," Ham comments.

"Hey—you think I could look around?"

Ham shrugs. "Sure."

They walk through the house, through the downstairs rooms and to the moldy basement, where Dad's old work bench is. "I'd forgot Dad used to do woodwork."

"He got me into it," Ham comments.

"Did he?"

"Yeah. I do restoration mostly. Antiques. I've had a few people bring me some pieces to rework."

"Maybe you oughta go into it professionally. You know, start a business."

"I've looked into it. I don't think I could make much money. Certainly not what I'm making now."

Bruce blows on his coffee and drinks. "More to life than money."

"Yeah, like bills."

Bruce nods. "True."

Upstairs, Bruce follows him through the bedrooms—through Dad's spartan quarters and Ham's old room, now jumbled with dusty boxes and discarded furniture. Then they open the door to Bruce's room, and Bruce wanders in, as if in a daze. Dust lies like carpet on everything, but Bruce doesn't seem to notice. He is staring at the walls, at the posters he taped up that still hang there—Poison, Motley Crue, Bon Jovi. He steps over a box of musty books and peeks through the curtain at the view from the window. "This is so weird," he says, "coming back in here after all this time." He looks back at Ham. "It seems so small."

His eyes light up. "Hey, I just thought of something." He squats and lifts up the bedspread, peering into the darkness and dust. "It's here. Oh, my God, it's here." He starts shoving boxes and piles of old magazines back out of the way. "Help me, Ham."

"What have you got under there?" Ham asks, taking a pile of yellowed newspapers from Bruce and shoving them into another corner.

Bruce pulls something flat from beneath the bed. Whatever it is, it's big and covered with a moldy sheet. "I can't believe this," Bruce says.

"What is it?"

Bruce pulls the sheet off. "My train."

Ham looks at the layout, at the intricate model buildings, at the streetlights, the little cars, the tiny people frozen in their tracks on the sidewalks. In a few moments, Bruce has found the cord, and he shoves aside a box and plugs it into an outlet. The layout comes to life with light and motion. The train begins moving around the oval of track, pulling a string of lighted passenger cars.

"I can't believe this thing still works," Ham says.

Bruce is laughing with joy. "Neither can I." He is watching the train, hypnotized. "I put this together in high school—over twenty years ago."

"You built this?" Ham says.

"Uh-huh. Took me months."

Ham studies the scenery—the little apple trees and ponds. There is even a farm with cows and horses. "I'm impressed," he says, meaning it.

Bruce looks up. "Are you?" He looks like a little boy sitting on the floor, his legs crossed, his face radiant with happiness. A boy and his train.

2

Christina sits in the silence of Ham's house, staring out at the back yard. Everything is brown and dead. Only a patch or two of dirty snow remains.

Kipp has already left. Soon after Christina arrived, Kipp was up and out the door, roaring away in his Mazda. He never said a word, and that's fine with her. She looks at her watch. She can't imagine where he would be going before ten-thirty. It's Black Friday, but she's fairly certain he wasn't going Christmas shopping.

Part of her wants to go back to his room, to search some more. Part of her wants to see that book again. But as soon as she thinks that, queasiness fills her stomach. Why? My God, she's as sick as Kipp is.

In the bathroom, she grabs the clothes hamper and drags it toward the laundry room off the kitchen. She really should help out, she thinks. The laundry used to be Kipp's job. But that was before. Before he changed. Now Ham has taken it upon himself to assume Kipp's chores. She wonders what Ham is thinking, letting Kipp get away with all this. To her knowledge, he hasn't said a word to Kipp about his coming and going, about his shunning of his duties. He is letting the boy do as he pleases. And maybe that is what is wrong with him.

Christina starts pulling clothes out of the hamper, sorting them into piles. Maybe Ham is afraid of him. Afraid to confront him. But why? He is Kipp's father, for God's sake. It is his duty to correct his son. His duty as a man.

She picks up a pair of Kipp's jeans, and she hears

something crinkle in the pocket. Her heart is pounding. She reaches in and pulls out a plastic bag. Loose pot. A few ready-made joints. Three or four unidentifiable pills. She drops the bag on top of the dryer and looks at it.

She is really not surprised to see it. Not surprised at all.

3

Kipp and Brett are parked behind the mall next to a dumpster. The sun is streaming into the car, and it feels like a greenhouse in there. Kipp cracks his window and a whiff of garbage wafts in. "Man, that stinks," Brett comments.

They are waiting for a man named Jesus. Jesus is dark and spindly, and he has a scraggly beard and ratty long hair. In the summer he doesn't wear a shirt, and his nipples are bared, showing how they stretch painfully over his ribs and the silver hoops with which they are pierced. On his stomach is a tattoo of a golden-haired Valkyrie riding a raging dragon. Jesus sells stuff.

"I can't believe you lost your weed," Brett says.

"I wouldn't have if I could just keep it in one place. But I don't trust that bitch Christina."

Brett is smoking a cigarette. He blows out a puff of smoke and Kipp's eyes burn. Strange how cigarette smoke bothers him but weed smoke doesn't. "She's bad news," Brett says. "You oughta find some way to teach her a lesson."

"Yeah," Kipp says, and he remembers his fantasy of Angela and Amber. Of using his knife. "She could use a good lesson."

Someone knocks on the window. It is Jesus. Kipp rolls down the glass. "You're late," he tells him.

"Sorry, man," he says, and his breath smells like shit. "There was a cop hangin' around."

"Where?"

"He's gone."

Kipp looks at the bulge in Jesus' coat pocket. "Whatcha got?"

Jesus pulls out a plastic bag. The weed is green and seedy. It looks like freshly-mown grass. "Pure Colombian," he says. He grins, showing his black teeth. "Primo."

"No shit?" Kipp says.

"Just got it in from a guy in Nashville. He just came back from Florida."

"How much?"

"Sell you the whole bag for seventy-five."

"You gotta be shitting me," Kipp tells him. "Fifty's all I can give you."

"Seventy."

"Sixty."

"Sixty-five."

"All right." Kipp pulls three twenties and a five out of his wallet and passes them to Jesus. Jesus drops the bag into the car, into Kipp's lap.

"Got somethin' else. If you're interested." He pulls another small bag out of his pocket. "Wanna buy some coke?"

Kipp looks at the white powder glistening in the package. He licks his lips.

"Pure stuff," Jesus says. He holds the bag out. "Wanna sample?"

"Yeah," Kipp whispers.

Jesus pinches a bit of the coke between his dirt-stained fingers and holds it out under Kipp's nose. Kipp inhales. And he feels his brain expand. And he is almost floating. The pleasure flows through him. He can feel it spreading through his veins. It feels like his bloodstream is having an orgasm. He looks at Brett. Brett looks so small and powerless. "Try some," he tells him, and Brett shakes his head. Brett's eyes are wide. What a fucking pussy. "How much?" Kipp asks Jesus.

"Hundred."

Kipp pulls out a hundred-dollar-bill and passes it wordlessly to Jesus. Jesus drops a bag in his lap.

Jesus' eyes sparkle and his slimy tongue runs across his scaly lips. "Nice doing bizness with ya, man." And then he is gone.

Kipp pops on his sunglasses and starts the car. Brett is still staring at him. "What the fuck you looking at?" Kipp asks him.

4

Ham has finally found Dad's insurance policy in a dresser drawer in the bedroom. Fifty thousand dollars in term life. Taken out in 1962. Bruce supposes that was a lot of money in those days, and Dad probably thought he would be providing amply for his family. But now with all of Dad's money, it seems kind of funny.

The policy was with a copy of Dad's will. The will names Dad's attorney as executor. The terms of the will specify that everything is to be divided between Ham and Bruce.

When Bruce reads that, when he sees it spelled out

before him, he almost weeps. And he is not sure why. Gratitude, certainly. But also sorrow. Relief. Excitement. This money will change his way of life forever. He'll never have to worry about paying bills or car repairs or his credit card debts again. But everything has a price. And he knows that the price of his financial freedom is the loss of his father. Just as he was beginning to know him again. Just as he was making a start of burying the hate he had harbored for that man for so long. Just as he was thinking that, maybe, his father had forgiven him; that maybe, seeing Bruce involved in a real, honest relationship, Dad might have begun to feel a little proud of his younger son. And now all of that is stopped cold and dead.

"You okay, Bruce?" Ham asks.

Bruce nods. "Yeah." He laughs humorlessly. "I just really never expected to be in the will," he says, and then wishes he hadn't.

Ham gives him a puzzled look. "Well, of course you'd be in the will. You were his son, too."

"I know."

"Why did you think that?"

"I don't know."

"Because you were in prison? Did you think Dad would disown you because you had served time?"

Bruce feels his face growing red. "Well. . . "

Ham shakes his head. "Holy shit, Bruce."

Bruce feels anger welling up in his belly. "Well, you know, the two of you haven't exactly given me the red carpet of welcome in the past few years. You both shunned me like I was dogshit."

Ham's brow tightens in annoyance. "C'mon, Bruce, you know that's not true."

"It's not, huh?" Bruce blows out a breath, looking away. "You never called, never came by to see me. The first time you speak to me in fifteen years is when you call to tell me our father's dying."

"Streets and phone lines run two ways, Bruce."

Bruce chews on his lip, too angry to say anything.

"In all those years, did you ever call to check on Dad? Did you ever come by to see him? What about all those holidays that went by—all those birthdays and Christmases and Father's Days—all those times you could have just sent him a goddamned card?" Ham sighs and gets to his feet. "So don't get all bent outa shape thinking that we had something to do with how fucking miserable you are. Everything that's happened to you is your fault."

"That's not true," Bruce whispers, and he can feel hot tears coursing down his face.

Ham's face is red with anger. "Then tell me why, man. Tell me why it's my fault you didn't call Dad for so long. Tell me why it's my fault you're so damned unhappy. And tell me why it's my fault you went to jail and fucked up your life. It sure as hell wasn't me that raped somebody."

"That's enough," Bruce says. He wipes his eyes. "You or Dad neither one ever asked me to tell my side of that story. All you know is what you heard in court. And Dad's precious lawyer—the first time I met with him, he was talking about pleading guilty to reduce the sentence before he even let me say a word. It's like none of you believed I was innocent. You believed some stupid sorority slut you'd never met over your own flesh and blood. I never even got to testify for chrissakes."

Ham flops down on their father's bed. "All right. So tell me. Let me hear all about it. Tell me how that girl lied and how she was really all over you to fuck her brains out."

Bruce looks at him. "You still don't believe I was innocent, do you?" Ham says nothing, and Bruce nods. "All right. Here's what happened. Pamela and I were in a class together. She sat beside me, and we used to flirt all the time. Sometimes our flirting would get pretty explicit. Sexually, I mean. Suggestive. There were all these little innuendoes."

"She did it too?"

"Yes. Even though at the trial she turned it around and said I harassed her sexually. It never happened like that. I swear."

"Okay. So you finally went out with her?"

Bruce nods. "Yeah. I finally asked her out. We went and got a pizza and then we went to a movie— some bad Kurt Russell flick. We were having a really good time. And the whole night, we had kept up that sex talk—just kind of a running thing. Just really suggestive."

"So you thought she was hot for you."

"No, not exactly. But we did wind up in her dorm room. Her roommate was out, and we had the place to ourselves. And one thing led to another. We'd been drinking. A lot. And we were making out—kissing and feeling, you know. And she passed out."

"And then?"

Bruce nods. "I left her there. Went home and fell asleep. But the next morning these two cops showed up at my door. Woke me up. They asked me who I was, and when I told them, they told me I was under arrest for rape. I laughed. And I was thinking the whole time that it was some kind of elaborate joke. I was in a fraternity, and I thought maybe those guys had planned the whole thing. But then the cops started reading me my rights. And they put me in handcuffs. And they led me to the police car. And when they brought me to the police station, I knew then that it was for real."

Ham is staring at the floor. "But why would she lie, Bruce? Why would she have done such a thing?"

Bruce shrugs. "Who knows. Maybe she just assumed that I took advantage of her being passed out. Or maybe she knew we were wealthy and she thought it would be a way to get her hands on some money."

Ham is shaking his head. "But I still don't understand. If you were innocent, why didn't you make Dad's lawyer put you on the witness stand? Why didn't you make him get your side out in the open?"

Bruce is staring blankly at the window. "I was a kid, Ham. I was barely twenty-one. I was scared shitless. He told me to let him handle it. That he would see that everything was okay. He told me to keep my mouth shut and try to look dignified. And of course I believed him."

Ham blows out a breath. "And all this time, I thought he wouldn't let you testify because he didn't want you to incriminate yourself."

"I'm sure that's what he was thinking, too."

"So he never asked you if you were innocent?"

Bruce shakes his head. "Nope."

Ham gives him a puzzled look. "But you could have appealed."

"I know." Bruce looks at him. "Dad wouldn't even consider it. He told me the family had been through enough. He said it was time you all got on with your lives and I took my punishment."

"He said that to you?"

"Yes."

Ham looks at the floor. "I'm sorry, Bruce. I really am."

"Why didn't you believe me?"

"I don't know." Ham blows out a breath. "I mean, I was married, I had a new baby, a good job. And rape just seemed so. . . heinous to me. I guess I just felt bad for that girl. You and I were never exactly close."

"That's true."

"And I didn't really know much about you. Your character. I had no idea whether you were capable of doing something like that or not." Ham looks at him. "But I am sorry about all of it. Believe me, I am." He looks away, to the bare tree limbs that are scratching against the window pane. "Does Kelly know?"

Bruce swallows. "No."

Ham looks back at him. "You haven't told her?"

"Not yet. I don't know what to do. I'm in so deep with her already. I never expected things to get this far. I never wanted to let them get this far."

"You've got to tell her."

"I know."

"Does she know about your inheritance?"

Bruce looks at him. "How could she? I didn't know about it myself 'til just now."

Ham stands and picks up the papers on the bureau. "Well, I guess I'd better get back home. I'll take these papers down to the lawyer first thing Monday morning. It shouldn't take too long to settle the estate. Then I suppose we can decide what to do about Dad's personal effects and his real estate." He walks around the room, blowing dust off the furniture. "I guess the best thing would be to sell the house and divide the money."

Bruce nods. "Yeah."

Ham looks back at him. "Hey, I just thought of something. Aren't you renting a trailer now?"

"Yeah."

"Would you want to move in here? I mean, we own it now, and there's no sense in you paying rent when you could live here for free."

Bruce looks at him. "You'd let me do that?"

Ham shrugs. "Sure. It's half yours. I already have a house. I don't need another one."

Bruce reels a bit. All of this is so overwhelming. So much at one time. Gratitude fills him once more, and his eyes brim with fresh tears. "Thank you, Ham."

FOURTEEN

1

Ham locks the front door of Dad's house and steps off the porch toward his car. Bruce left a few minutes ago, and Ham stayed behind to sit in Dad's easy chair and think. To ponder.

That poor, miserable son-of-a-bitch. His life has been completely ruined. And all because of that girl's lie. And she waltzed away with the two hundred thousand dollars of Dad's money the court awarded her. Hell, she ruined all their lives. The publicity almost devastated Dad's company. And it most certainly stunted Ham's financial career.

What hurts Ham the most is the fact that he never allowed himself to believe Bruce was innocent. He remembers that Sunday morning when the phone woke him, and Dad, on the other end, told him simply, "Bruce is in trouble. He raped a girl." Just like that. Not, "A girl claims Bruce raped her." How is it that his and Dad's relationship with Bruce could get to that point? To the point where they didn't know if they could believe Bruce or not?

Ham still can't believe Dad's lawyer wouldn't let Bruce on the witness stand in his own defense. Of course the prosecution had torn his character apart, twisting his actions and portraying him as a spoiled rich brat who was used to getting everything he wanted—especially sex. They had even tracked down Bruce's girlfriend from high school—a girl named Lee Ann—and questioned her extensively about her sexual experiences with Bruce. And through all of it, Dad sat passively, watching as if it were some damned TV show. Ham can't understand Dad letting his attorney treat Bruce that way. My God, how quickly a person's life can get fucked up.

Ham turns onto Main Street, passing the bank and the storefronts. The city has put up Christmas decorations—huge lines of snowflakes that span over the street between the buildings—and the cold morning sun sparkles on the glitter and tinsel. God, how he hates the holidays.

He pulls into his drive behind Christina's BMW, surprised that she is already here. He grabs the papers and heads for the door.

Inside, he can smell laundry detergent and Lysol. Christina is cleaning house. He smiles a little to himself; she's never been one to tolerate disorder.

He rounds the corner to the kitchen and sees her scrubbing on the stove. "Hey," he says.

At the sound of his voice, she jumps and screams, then leans back against the counter. "You scared me."

"Sorry." He steps over to kiss her ear. "You've been busy."

She nods. "You know me."

"Kipp gone already?"

"Yes."

"Kinda early, isn't it? For Kipp?"

She shrugs. "Come here. I have something to show you." She leads him to the laundry room. She points to the top of the dryer, and Ham sees the bag of drugs. At first he is stunned. Then angry. "I found it in one of his pockets," Christina is saying.

Ham picks it up, examining the pills through the loose pot. "Damn."

Christina looks at him. "You've got to talk to him again, Ham. Something has to change."

"I know."

"It just can't go on like this. He's going to hurt somebody."

"I *know*." He pitches the bag down and shoves his hands in his pockets. "Damn," he says again.

* * *

At four o'clock, just as the light outside is beginning to fade, Kipp pulls up in the driveway.

Christina left an hour ago, afraid to witness the confrontation. Ham has been sitting here ever since, pretending to watch a University of Kentucky football game. He realizes he is nervous, and it angers him that he has allowed Kipp to make him afraid.

Kipp's keys rattle in the door, and Ham hears his light footsteps in the foyer. "Kipp?"

"Yeah."

"C'mere."

Kipp shuffles into the den, and for the first time in weeks, Ham is looking at him—really *looking*—at him. And he is shocked. Kipp looks emaciated and fragile—weak. He looks just like Hamilton Senior did when he got sick. "Sit down," Ham tells him.

Kipp flops down on the sofa. "What is it?"

Ham picks up the bag of drugs from between his legs and tosses it to Kipp. It lands in Kipp's lap, and Kipp stares at it, his face turning red. "Where did you get this?" Kipp mutters.

"Tell me about it," Ham says.

"What do you mean?"

"I want to know all about that. Where it came from. Who sold it to you. How much more you've got hidden somewhere." Kipp stares at the bag, not saying anything. Ham is trying hard to suppress the rising rage. "Goddammit, Kipp. We had a deal. You said you weren't going to do that shit anymore."

"I guess I lied."

"Yes, I guess you did." Ham looks away. "When's it gonna stop, son? Look at yourself. You look bad. Sick. You've got a problem."

Kipp blows out a breath. "Can I go now?"

Anger stabs Ham's gut. "No, sir, you cannot. This shit has got to stop. All this coming and going at all hours, shirking your chores. And this goddamned attitude of yours. I'm sick of it. It stops now."

Kipp is fingering the bag. "I suppose Christina found this."

Ham looks at him. Blinks. "Yes. It was in the pocket of your jeans. She was doing laundry. Which, I might add, is supposed to be your job."

"Did she tell you she went through my room?" Kipp says, not looking at him. "Did she tell you she snooped through my closet and all my drawers?"

Ham's stomach is burning. "Yes, she did." He blows out a breath. "She told me what she found."

Kipp's face is fiery red. He looks at Ham, and the cold in Kipp's eyes sends chills up the back of Ham's neck. "What gives her the right to do that? To look through all my stuff?"

"Tell me about the knife, Kipp. The dagger."

Kipp is standing now. "It's *my stuff*. My *private* stuff. It's none of her goddamned business."

"That's enough," Ham says, getting to his feet. "She's just concerned about you. We're *both* concerned."

Kipp looks at him squarely. "Yeah? Well, it seems to me your girlfriend is a goddamned little sneak."

Before Ham realizes what he is doing, he sees his hand fly out, and he slaps Kipp across the face. Kipp reels back, falling onto the sofa. He puts his hand to his cheek, pulls it away, looks at it. Ham is suddenly ashamed. "Kipp, I'm sorry."

Kipp is looking at Ham in disbelief. "You hit me." Tears are welling up in his eyes. "You *hit* me." He gets to his feet, running toward the front door. "Mother fucker!" he gasps through choking sobs. "Mother *fucker!*"

"Kipp! Come back here!" The door slams, and he hears Kipp's Mazda roar to life, then squeal off down the street. Ham sinks back into his chair. Drained.

2

The herbal tea that Christina bought at the shop on Seventh Street is not doing its job. The clerk told her chamomile would be calming. Soothing. This is her second cup, and she is still nervous. So when her phone rings on the table beside her, she jumps and grabs it before it can ring a second time.

"It's me," Ham says on the other end.

"What happened?" she asks, breathless.

Ham blows out a breath. "I did it. I talked to him again."

"How'd it go?"

"Not too well. I lost my temper. I slapped him."

"Oh, Ham," she says, disappointed.

"I know. He left a few minutes ago. I'm just worried sick."

"Any idea where he might be?"

"No. Probably running around town somewhere. I just hope he doesn't do something stupid."

"Have you tried calling any of his friends?"

"I tried Brett's house, but nobody answered and I don't know his cell."

Guilt has settled over Christina like a net; the harder she tries to fight it, the more tangled in it she becomes. "Should we try to go look for him?"

"I don't know. I'm afraid to go chasing after him."

"What about the police? Have you called them?"

"I thought about that, too. But I don't want to make him any madder than he is already."

She leans back against the chair. "I'm sorry, honey."

"Nothing for you to feel sorry about."

"I just feel. . . responsible somehow."

"It's not your fault, Chris."

"I guess not." She looks at the ceiling. "So what do we do now?"

"I don't know. Wait for him to come home, I suppose."

"I love you."

"I love you, too, baby."

"You call me the minute you find out something."

"I will."

She hangs up the phone. Beside her, the tea has

grown cold.

3

Fuck, Kipp thinks.

Earlier, right after he left the house, he drove to the overgrown parking lot of an abandoned grocery. From beneath his seat, he pulled out his algebra book and set it on the console beside him. In his coat pocket, he found the bag of coke. He opened it and sifted some of it out onto the book. Then he took his pocket knife and gently cut the mound into two lines. Then he rolled up a five-dollar bill, stuck one end into his nostril and inhaled. And that's when he realized that he didn't have coke after all. He had a bag full of fucking baking soda. That cocksucker Jesus had screwed him over.

This has been one hell of a day. That bitch Christina is going to pay. Oh, yes. When he gets through with her, they won't be able to tell her mouth from her asshole. But first he's going to take care of Jesus.

Beside him now, Brett sits slumped in the passenger seat. "What're you gonna do when you find him?" he asks.

Kipp grins. "I'm gonna do 'im, man. Do him real good."

But after cruising through town and around the mall for over an hour, there is still no sign of him. No one has seen him, not even the black junkies in Peace Park, the ones that lurk around the dilapidated bandstand.

"I'm gonna find that son-of-a-bitch," Kipp mutters. "And he will pay. There's no fucking way I'm letting him get away with this. No fucking way."

Brett pops open another beer. "C'mon, man, have

a Bud. Let's go down to the Road. You can drink a Bud and chill. You need to relax, man."

Kipp slaps the beer from Brett's hands, and Brett grabs it up before it all spills out. "Go fuck yourself," Kipp tells him.

"What's the matter with you?" Brett says.

Then Kipp sees the girl. She is walking along the edge of the road. Probably about thirteen, wearing a red rain slicker. Yellow-haired and skinny. Ugly. He presses on the accelerator and the car speeds up.

Brett catches sight of her. "What're you doin'?"

Kipp turns the wheel, aiming for her. "Just runnin' down another dog," he says.

The girl has spotted them now. She stands frozen in the lights like a deer.

"Jesus, man!" Brett cries. He grabs the steering wheel and the car swerves away from her, missing her by inches. Kipp pushes him away, jerking the steering wheel. The car spins around, sliding on the pavement. Headlights flash on them, illuminating Brett's white face, and a pickup truck swerves around them, horn blaring. After an eternity, the car stops.

Brett sinks back into the seat. "Jesus Christ, Kipp! What the hell did you do that for?"

Kipp shifts into first and peals out back down the road. "You're such a pussy," Kipp tells him.

"You could've killed her!" Brett screams. "You could've killed *us!*" He blows out a breath, wiping the sweat off his forehead. "You've got a problem, man. You are sick."

Kipp slams on the brakes, and Brett is thrown forward, his seat belt catching him around the neck. Kipp feels under his seat until his fingers find what they are searching for. He brings the pistol out and cocks it, pointing it at Brett's head.

"Jesus, man!"

"Get out," Kipp tells him.

Brett looks at him incredulously. "What?"

"Get the fuck out of my car."

Brett unbuckles his seat belt, eyeing Kipp cautiously. He eases open the door. "You need help, man."

"Get *out!*" Kipp screams.

Brett slides out of the car and slams the door. Kipp roars away, leaving Brett standing in the street gaping after him.

4

Bruce can feel his heart pounding frantically. The time has come, he knows, to tell Kelly the truth. A few minutes ago he called her to let her know he was coming over, and she was pleased. So here he stands on her front step, the guilt thudding thickly through his body.

He taps on the door, and inside he hears Amanda yell excitedly, "Bruce! It's Bruce!" Kelly opens the door, and Bruce greets her with a kiss. "Hi," she says.

"Hi."

Amanda is in her high chair picking at a plate of chicken nuggets and overdone french fries. "Hi, Bruce."

"Hi, Amanda."

"I'm watching *Snow White*."

"You are?"

"Uh-huh. That old woman just gave her an apple."

"Oh."

Kelly rolls her eyes. "I'm sick of this movie," she says. She ushers Bruce over to the sofa. "You had dinner?"

"Yeah."

"Want some coffee?"

"Sure. That sounds good."

Kelly bends down and rubs her nose against his. "Cold outside?"

"Very." He watches her disappear into the kitchen. This is not a good time to spring this on her, he thinks. Maybe later.

On the screen, the dwarfs have put Snow White into a glass coffin. "Is she dead?" Amanda asks.

"No," Bruce tells her. "Just sleeping."

* * *

Later, after Bruce helps Amanda brush her teeth and gives her a bedtime kiss and Kelly has tucked her in and said goodnight, Bruce knows the time has come. He sits down on the sofa, and Kelly slides in beside him, propping her feet against the edge of the coffee table. She snuggles against his chest. "What do you wanna do now?" she asks seductively.

Bruce's stomach burns. "We need to talk," he tells her.

"You sound serious," she says, looking up at him.

"I am."

She sits up, not taking her gaze off him. "What's the matter?"

He takes a deep breath and blows it out slowly. "How much do you know about me being in prison?"

She blinks, then looks away. "I know you served time. That's about all."

"So you don't know what I was in for?"

"No." She looks back at him. "Are you gonna tell me you killed somebody or something?"

"Not exactly."

"What is it, Bruce?"

He looks at the floor. "I was accused of rape."

He launches into his story—all of it, just the way he told Ham, not stopping to look at her. When he is finished, she says nothing. Bruce glances at her and sees tears sliding silently down her cheeks. "Why didn't you tell me sooner?" she says.

"I tried," he tells her. "I. . . I just couldn't. I never wanted things to go so far." He leans his head on the back of the sofa, staring at the ceiling. "I'm sorry, Kelly," he says. "I never wanted to hurt you. I was just . . . well, never sure about how to tell you. But I was innocent. You have to believe that."

He reaches for her hand and she pulls it away, then looks at him apologetically. "I'm sorry, Bruce," she says. She takes his hand. "It's just so much to throw at me all of a sudden."

"You believe me, don't you? About me being innocent?"

She looks away, wiping her eyes. "I don't know."

He squeezes her hand. "Kelly, you've got to believe me. I didn't rape that girl. I swear." He suddenly feels desperate. He is holding her as if by doing so he can change her mind, as if he can make everything just like it was a few minutes ago before he told her. "I love you, Kelly," he says. And then he wishes he hadn't. "I haven't said that to anybody in a long time. And I hadn't been with anybody since. . . " His voice trails off; he was about to say "since prison," but thought better of it.

Kelly pulls her hand away again. "I think you ought to go now, Bruce." She looks at him. "I need some time to think. To be by myself."

He looks at the floor, at Amanda's Barbies

scattered across the worn brown carpet. "All right."

She blows out a breath. "I'm sorry. I guess I just need to digest all of it."

"It's okay," he says. "I understand." He is trying hard to keep his voice from cracking. "I'll give you all the time you need."

"I'm just. . . confused."

"I know." He stands, watching her. "I'll let myself out."

"Okay."

"Goodnight."

"Bye."

He steps out into the crisp air and pulls the door to gently. Tears slide down his face, cold and stinging. He climbs into his car and sits there a moment, looking at the apartment complex, at all the Christmas trees lighted in the windows.

"Fuck," he says.

* * *

At the trailer, Sherwin runs to greet him, rubbing against his legs and purring. Bruce reaches down and scratches him between the ears. He unlocks the door, and Sherwin slips inside, making for the chair in the corner where he plops down and proceeds to bathe.

Bruce grabs a beer from the refrigerator and makes his way back to the bedroom. The beer is cold, and it bubbles in his stomach like molten sulfur.

From his closet he pulls a gay porn magazine called *Inches* and a bottle of mineral oil. He masturbates quickly, furiously, barely feeling his orgasm. His head is swimming, and a cold sweat has beaded up on his forehead. He runs to the bathroom, barely making it to the toilet before he vomits up the beer. Still naked, he sinks to the floor and wipes his mouth on a hand towel. God, how he hates this.

He doesn't want this. He doesn't want to end up seventy years old and masturbating to pictures of naked men. He doesn't want to be gay, but doesn't want to be alone, either. He wants a woman. A real woman. He wants Kelly.

He climbs to his feet and shuffles back to the bedroom and crawls into his clothes. He opens the closet door and pulls out a stack of magazines. All of them porn, all of them gay.

He takes the magazines to the kitchen and proceeds to rip them apart, one by one, pretending not to see the fragments of erect penises and muscled chests, the website ads promising unparalleled pleasure. All of the scraps he shoves into a garbage bag which he ties with a wire strip. He slips on his shoes and steps back into the night air.

It's a sacrifice, he thinks. A burnt offering. For Kelly. He will show God just how much he wants to change. How much he wants to be with the woman he loves. How much she means to him.

At the edge of the trailer park, he flings the bag into the garbage dumpster. Sometimes raccoons get into the trash, and he smiles, thinking what Andre and the others would do if they came outside one morning to discover these pictures scattered all over their front yards. He thinks what Gary would do, and his blood runs cold. But none of that will happen.

Back inside, he kicks off his shoes and flops onto the sofa. Sherwin is still in the chair, but now he is asleep, purring contentedly.

Bruce smiles.

FIFTEEN

1

It has been one hell of a Monday.

Saturday night, after Ham had worried himself into a frenzy, Kipp finally came home about midnight. He stood in the foyer, and he and Ham eyed each other for a moment, neither saying a word. Then Kipp headed down the hall toward his room, and Ham heard him lock the door. Then the bass thud of Kipp's stereo pounded through the house. But at least he was home. Ham stood outside Kipp's door for a long time, wondering what he was doing in there, and then feeling grateful that he didn't know. But sleep had been a long time in coming.

And then, after being off for a few days and the usual backlog from a holiday, Ham was overwhelmed by the amount of work piled up on his desk at eight o'clock this morning. There were at least ten loan folders waiting for him, two interoffice memos, sixteen voice mails, a stack of mail three inches thick, and over fifty emails. He looks at his watch: three-thirty. He skipped lunch, but his desk doesn't look much better.

Kay taps lightly on the door and pokes her head inside. "Mr. Ham?"

"What is it, Miss Kay?"

She slips in through the door. "Mr. Tate wants to see you," she whispers. "In his office."

Ham blows out a breath. Ben Tate is such a prick. He never ignores a chance to remind Ham that he is over ten years younger and already president of the bank; it is a title which he seems to regard as the banking industry's equivalent of knighthood. "What does he want?" Ham asks.

"I don't know. But he didn't look too happy. His face was red."

Ham looks at the financial reports in his hand and then tosses them on his desk. "Shit," he mutters.

He steps around the corner to the door of Ben's office. "Whatcha need?"

Ben looks up. "Come on in, Ham. Close the door." He nods toward the chair across the desk. "Have a seat."

Ham sits down uneasily, his knuckles white as he grasps the arms of the chair. "What's going on?"

Ben leans back in his big chair. "How're you doing?"

"Fine." He despises Ben when he tries to make small talk. Ben has never been good at it; it's so fake, so contrived.

"Sorry I didn't make it to your dad's funeral," he says. "I was out of town."

"That's all right," Ham tells him, meaning it. The last thing he had wanted to see last Thursday was Ben's big ass parked up there in the funeral home. "We appreciated the flowers, though."

Ben nods. He scratches at his scalp through his thin red hair, then swipes his hand across his pudgy cheek and adjusts his glasses. "Ham, let me get right to the point. I understand all you've been going through the past few weeks with your father being sick and all. I've tried to overlook a lot of things. All your absences and taking off work early and everything. I really hope we're through with all that."

Ham is losing the battle against the scowl he feels forming on his face. He can't believe this prick is saying this to him. "I hope I'm through with it, too, Ben. It hasn't been easy, you know."

"I understand that." He sighs. "I just hope you know what a bind it put the rest of us in. You know, we're a team here. A family. And we can't function correctly if everybody's not pulling his own weight."

Ham feels his face growing red with anger. His stomach burns and his jaw is working frantically. "I understand, Ben," he says evenly. "But it's not like I could help all this."

Ben is scratching his eyebrow. "Just seems to me like your brother could have helped you with some of it. So you wouldn't have had to miss so much work."

Ham looks toward the window. "Bruce didn't even know Dad was sick for a long time."

Ben looks at him. "You didn't tell him?"

"Bruce and I haven't exactly been close." He looks back at Tate. "But after he found out, he did help some."

Tate looks at his desk. "You know, I'm not one to meddle in someone else's family affairs, but it seems like your brother's been taking advantage of you."

Ham stares at him. "Why do you say that?"

Tate shrugs, scratching his head. He really needs some dandruff shampoo, Ham thinks. "Well," Ben says, "he doesn't have a family. It looks like he could have offered to take care of your dad instead of you having to move him into your house."

"He hadn't even seen our dad in several years," Ham says. "It would've been like taking in a total stranger."

Ben dismisses all of it with a wave of his hand. "Well, whatever. You know him better than I do. I've just seen too many people stay out of their family's lives and then waltz back in just in time to pick up their inheritance. Then they're gone again. Happens all the time. I'm just trying to prepare you for that."

"Bruce is not that kind of guy," Ham says. He realizes suddenly that he is defending Bruce, something he never expected to be doing. "Whatever Bruce has done since he got out of prison is what he's had to do to survive. My father didn't exactly welcome him back with open arms. It's only natural that Bruce has been kind of distant. But he has made it by himself. And with all the obstacles he's had to face, I'd say that's doing pretty damned good." Ham looks at Tate squarely. "You can't expect a man to come running to a family that's shunned him. Even when he's desperate."

Tate holds up his hands. "All right, all right. Calm down. I didn't mean to step on anybody's toes."

"Well, I don't see as how any of it is your business," Ham says before he can stop himself. "I mean, I'm getting my job done. That's all that should matter to you."

Tate nods. "Well, let's just hope we don't have any more family emergencies."

Ham looks at Ben, thinking what an arrogant little prick he is. "Yes. Let's hope." He storms out of Ben's office and into his own, not meeting Kay's eyes, and slams his door. He sinks into his chair. He is shaking with anger.

2

The time has come, Christina thinks. She pulls into Ham's driveway behind Kipp's car. It is time somebody stood up to Kipp. Time to show him he can't lord over everyone and get away with it. And if Ham isn't going to do it, by God, she is going to.

She hesitates on the steps. My God, what is she doing? She thinks about that dagger, about the sickness of Kipp's soul, about those horrible magazines with their pages stiff with dried semen. She is terrified, she realizes. Kipp might do anything to her. And she wonders if she should have brought a weapon. Something—anything at all—with which to defend herself.

Just inside the door, she can hear the television blasting MTV, and the light is flashing and dizzying, like a strobe in the shadowy den. Slowly, she steps toward the sound until she can see Kipp. He is lying on the sofa in his underwear. His eyes are invisible behind the reflection of the television on his glasses. On the screen, a blond in leather is squirming to the squealing guitars and throat-tearing vocals. Christina spots the remote control and grabs for it, reeling with disorientation in the sudden quiet.

On the sofa, Kipp sits up and whirls around, his hands moving to cover his crotch. "What the fuck are you doing?" he spits. "Why are you sneaking around the house like that?"

"I wasn't sneaking," Christina says.

"Bullshit."

Christina's fear is giving way to anger. "You're the one who had the TV up so loud you couldn't hear anything else."

Kipp glares at her, then flops back down on the couch. "Turn it back on."

Christina tightens her grip on the remote. "No."

Kipp's gaze doesn't move from the blank screen. "Turn the goddamned TV back on."

Before her fear of him can crowd out her anger, she bends down and slaps him across the cheek. Hard. He sits up, looking at her in disbelief, his eyes watering. She tightens her jaw. "You don't ever talk to me that way."

"Who the fuck do you think you are?" he mutters. He rubs his face where the red palm-print is beginning to flare. "You come in here like you own the place, telling me what to do, hit me, go snooping through my room. . . You don't even live here. You're not my mother."

"I'm the closest you've got," she tells him. She realizes she is holding the remote like a club, ready to strike him if he moves toward her.

"I don't need a mother." He stands and starts toward the hall.

"Stop right there," she says, and surprisingly, he does, turning to look at her with the eyes of a snake. "I am damned sick and tired of you acting like this. I'm tired of you treating your father like this. After he does so much for you. And you pay him back by treating him this way."

"Give me a break," Kipp says, turning back around and heading for his room.

"Come here," Christina calls, but this time he doesn't turn around, and she hears the door slam shut.

She sighs and sinks into Ham's chair, tears blurring her vision. God, she needs a drink.

3

Kipp leans against his door, his heart pounding with anger and embarrassment. That fucking bitch. She had no right. *No right.* He reaches down and locks the door. Anger is gripping him like a vise. He swipes at the top of his chest of drawers, and papers, books, and trophies go flying across the room. His basketball award from last year for Most Improved Player smashes against the wall, leaving a dark streak. He picks it up and brings it crashing down against his night stand, breaking off the gold plastic figure of a perfect athlete crowned with a wreath of laurel. The figure lies on the floor like a dead body. Kipp stares at it for a moment. Then he remembers something.

In his closet, behind a loose section of drywall, is the hiding place his father and Christina have not seen. Inside is an ancient, scuffed-up brief case his father gave him to play with years ago. He pulls it out and stares at it. His heart is still pounding, but now it beats with sexual excitement. Already an erection is straining in his underwear. He opens the latches and flips up the lid. Inside is his stash of weed, his gun, and a book. He has not looked at this book in a long time, not much since he bought it from some freak off eBay. The name of it is *The Art of the Autopsy*.

Kipp flops down on the bed and begins to leaf through the pages. Picture after picture of corpses, aborted fetuses, and severed body parts. In the captions below the photographs, the author describes the wounds on the bodies and the causes of death. But Kipp rarely reads; mostly he stares at the photographs. There are victims of shootings, falls, drownings, accidents, and disease. But his favorite is the color photograph of the eighteen-year-old college girl, the one who was raped by four men and then strangled. An inset photograph shows a close-up of her vagina, all blue and bruised and bloody.

Kipp is looking at this picture now. His hand is creeping toward his erection. A strand of drool sinks slowly from the corner of his mouth and pools on the page.

4

Bruce pulls into the parking lot of Kelly's apartment complex. Her lights are on, glowing warmly in the growing dusk. He did not call before coming over, mostly because he was afraid she would tell him to stay away. He steps out of the car, shivering in the bitter wind. He feels like Vera Miles in *Psycho*, walking up the hill to the Bates mansion to confront Anthony Perkins. He can almost hear that creepy Bernard Herrmann music: *bum-da-da-dadum, bum-da-da-dadum.*

He knocks on the door, and he can hear her footsteps coming closer. The porch light blares on, and the door opens a crack. Kelly peeks out. The door is chained. "Oh, hi," she says. She closes the door and unlocks it, then opens it wide. "Come on in."

He steps into the warmth of the apartment, his frozen hands stuffed into his pockets. He looks at her awkwardly, longing to kiss her, to hold her, but he doesn't dare. "What's going on?" he says.

"Not much."

"Where's Amanda?"

She motions for him to sit down. "She's over at Mom's. I just got in from work. I wanted to change clothes before I went to pick her up."

From her expression, it is hard to tell what she is thinking. But her voice is distant and guarded. "I missed seeing you this weekend," he says, feeling his face grow red. "It sure was lonely."

She gives him a half-smile. "I know."

He looks around, the silence pressing on him. "So. You want to do something tonight?"

"Like what?"

"Go eat or something. We can pick up Amanda and go to a restaurant."

She looks away, staring at the floor. "I don't know, Bruce. I. . . I just don't think that's a good idea."

A sickening, desperate feeling sinks into his chest. "You don't?"

"No."

He looks at the portrait on the wall, the picture of Kelly and Amanda. "Oh." His eyes are burning. *I will not cry*, he thinks, *I will not cry*.

"I don't think we ought. . . to see each other for awhile."

Bruce swallows, trying to clear away that rising hurt. "All right."

"I'm just not comfortable with it."

"I understand."

She grabs his hand, making him jump. "I've just been sick about all this," she says. "Please understand. It's not you. I've really struggled with my feelings the past few days."

"I see."

She lets go and turns away. "I'm sorry."

"Me, too."

"We'll still be friends. We'll still see each other at work."

He shrugs. "I don't think so." He looks at her. "I've made a decision. This Friday is my last day at the Gas-N-Pack."

She glances at him. "Are you leaving?"

"I'm going back to school. This spring. I'm going to finish up my bachelor's."

"Oh, that's great. Where you going?"

"I haven't really decided yet, but probably back to Centre." He looks away. "I'll be through in a year. I'll have my degree in finance."

"Then what?"

He shrugs. "I'm not sure. We'll have to see what happens."

She sniffs, and Bruce realizes she is crying. "I'm really sorry about all this. I am."

"I'm sorry, too."

She looks at him, and her tear-streaked face is red and blotchy. "If you just knew how hard it was to think about all this. I. . . I've hardly slept since you told me."

"Yeah."

"I love you," she whispers, "but I just can't. . . you know. Not like before. Before you told me."

"Yeah," he says again, not knowing what else to say. He sits there for a moment, feeling crushed beneath the weight of the heavy silence. "I guess I'd better go. You need to go pick up Amanda. I need to get home and start packing."

She looks at him, puzzled. "Packing?"

"I'm moving. To my father's house."

"Oh." She follows him to the door. "Good luck, Bruce."

He turns and looks at her. "Thanks." He steps out into the stabbing air, pulling the door closed behind him.

* * *

He is halfway across town when the tears come. He is sitting numbly at a stoplight, not really thinking about anything, and he notices a tickling on his cheek. When he swipes at it, his fingertips come away wet. And when he realizes he is crying, the tears begin to pour.

It has happened to him again. Except this time he waited too long to tell. And now the cut, the separation, has more the feeling of a jagged tear instead of a clean amputation. It is over. Everything is over. All those hopes he had for Kelly and himself—gone. All the promise the relationship held, the promise of erasing his loneliness, of curing those confusing stirrings he felt inside—all of that has been wiped out. And he knows it won't be long before he is thinking about men again and wondering exactly what his feelings mean. It won't be long before he is looking at gay porn again and masturbating in feverish, filthy, sickening isolation.

But at least he has one thing to look forward to— finishing school. The decision to return to college was not a difficult one to make. As soon as he realized he would be inheriting all that money, he knew what he would do. The only question is whether he can get signed up in time. But if he can't get into school this coming spring semester, there's always next fall. But the point is, there's hope. And hope is all he has left.

He thought about staying on at the Gas-N-Pack for awhile, earning money to live on instead of spending his inheritance. But then he thought, why? What would be the point of staying on at a job he hates, working for a company that doesn't give a damn, not making much above minimum wage, when he will have close to three million dollars? It just didn't make sense. Not when the interest alone on that money could pay his living expenses.

He thinks about his father's house. *His* house now. He wonders what he will do with it. The inside is musty; it smells of stale cigars and Vic's Vap-O-Rub and old bacon grease. The walls are yellowed with age and dust. But there will be plenty of time to fix all that; plenty of time to do all that needs doing.

Yesterday he told Gary he would be moving at the end of the month. He just walked over to Gary's front door and knocked, and when Gary came to the door—sleepy or drunk, Bruce couldn't tell which—he simply said, "I'm moving next week." Gary nodded. Bruce said, "You can give my deposit back when I turn in my key." Then he left. Gary had not said a word. Bruce was glad; he braced himself all the way back home, waiting for a verbal assault that never came, half-expecting Gary to call him a fag again. But none of that happened. And thank God he'll never have to worry about that again. He and Sherwin can live out their days in peace and solitude.

Bruce smiles faintly through his tears. Sherwin's a good cat.

SIXTEEN

1

As soon as Ham sees Christina's face, he knows something is wrong. She meets him at the door, pale and red-eyed and shaking. "What's the matter, babe?" he asks her.

She pulls him inside. "It's Kipp," she whispers.

Ham's stomach suddenly burns. "What's he done now?"

She holds him, pressing her face against his chest. "I had a talk with him. We had a fight. I hit him."

He looks at her. "*You* hit him?"

"I slapped him." She sighs and stares into his eyes. "He made me so damned mad, Ham. You should've heard the way he talked to me."

Ham blows out a breath. "I can imagine." He kisses her forehead. "Are you okay?"

"I'm fine. Just upset."

"Where's Kipp?"

"In his room. He's been in there for over an hour now, and I haven't heard a sound out of him."

Ham looks down the dark hallway toward Kipp's door. "I wonder if I should try to talk to him."

"I'm sorry," Christina says. "I really am."

He kisses her again and slips out of his coat and jacket. "Nothing for you to be sorry about, honey." He shuffles down the hall to the shadowy corner where one thin line of light glows beneath Kipp's door. He taps lightly. "Kipp?"

"Go away."

"Why don't you come out, son, so we can talk?"

"Fuck you."

Ham stiffens with shock and anger. "Why are you acting like this?" he hisses. He tries the knob but it doesn't budge.

"Locked," Kipp informs him.

Rage boils in Ham's gut. He pounds his fists on the door. "Open up this goddamned door right *now*."

"Why can't you just leave me alone?" Kipp hollers. "I just want everybody to leave me the fuck alone. Can't you do that?"

"I'm worried about you, Kipp."

"Why?"

"Something's wrong with you. You're not acting like yourself. I'm afraid for you." *And* of *you*, he thinks. "Now come on out so we can talk like civilized men." He blows out a breath. "I want you to apologize to Christina."

Behind the door, Kipp laughs, and a chill crawls over Ham's scalp. "Apologize? You want *me* to apologize? She slapped me. She had no reason to."

"She said you talked back to her."

"So? She's not my goddamned mother. She can't tell me what to do."

Ham looks back up the hall. Christina leans against the wall with her head down, her arms folded across her chest. Ham faces the door. "Kipp, I expect you to treat her with respect, and to act like a decent human being." There is no answer. "Kipp?"

"What?"

Sweat has begun to trickle down Ham's forehead; he can feel it beading up above his eyebrows. "How do you think your mother would feel about this?"

For a moment there is silence behind the door. Then Ham hears a low chuckle that sends a chill rippling down the back of his neck. An image flashes before his eyes, some half-remembered vision from a long-ago Sunday school class of a horned Satan, his red skin aglow from the flames of Hell, his black eyes piercing through the smoke. "Come on out," Ham stammers. "Please."

"No."

Ham blows out an exasperated breath. "Come out of that room *now*."

Kipp's voice comes back clear and firm: "Leave me alone."

Ham stares at the door for a moment, and then the rage boils over. His fist slams into the thin wood, and he feels the door give a little. His hand explodes in pain. "Goddamn you, Kipp, you come out of that room right now or I'll break it down."

There is silence for a moment, and then icy fear grips Ham as Kipp says, "You do and I'll blow your fucking head off. I've got a gun." Kipp's voice is steady and calm.

Ham looks at the yellow glow from beneath Kipp's door, at the splintery dent where his own fist slammed home. "Shit," he whispers.

2

Christina watches Ham in the darkened hallway, watches him slump. Defeated. "What is it?" she says, coming up to him.

"He says he's got a gun."

Fear and anger grip her stomach. "Maybe—maybe he's lying."

"I don't know."

She reaches out and pecks on the door with her fingernails. "Kipp?"

"What the fuck do *you* want?"

The harshness of his voice stings, and she almost reels as if slapped. "I. . . I want to apologize. I shouldn't have hit you. I'm sorry."

Kipp laughs bitterly. "Fuck you."

Ham's fist bangs against the door frame. "God*dam*mit, Kipp. You do *not* talk to her like that."

"Get away from the door. Both of you."

Christina clutches Ham's arm. "Kipp, please."

Christina jumps as Kipp's door flies open. A skeleton stands before them, his hair sticking straight up as if from fright, his stomach heaving with his heavy breathing. "My God, Kipp. . . " Christina whispers.

Kipp's eyes are black as pitch. "I said get away from my fucking door." He raises his arm and points the gun. He fires.

3

It's been quiet now for a little while. Since he shot them. For a moment he couldn't look at them. He shot Christina through the head; the bullet struck her just above the left temple, and the back of her skull exploded, leaving a big swash of blood on the hallway wall. Ham did not utter a sound. Not even when Kipp pulled the trigger again and Ham's jaw disappeared in a spray of blood and bones.

He stares at them now where they lie in a mangled heap, their eyes wide open and blank. He steps back into his room and notices something warm and sticky on his leg. Looking down, he realizes he has had an orgasm; semen is dripping from his underwear and running down his thigh. He didn't even feel it.

He lies back on the bed. His ears still ring from the blast—a hollow hum. The gun is still warm in his hand. His heart is pounding, pounding like a drum. His whole body seems to pulse with each throb.

He stares up at the crack in his ceiling. "Well, Bugs, I think we've really fucked up this time."

On his bedside table is his bag of stuff. He digs out a joint and pops it between his lips. He tries to light it with a disposable lighter, but his hand is shaking so badly that the flame won't stand still. The lighter pops out of his grasp and falls to the floor. "Fuck." He leans over the side of the bed and picks it up with two fingers. This time he manages to light the joint and inhale deeply. After a minute, the shakes seem to let up, and he feels a bit calmer. He wipes his forehead, and his hand comes away dripping with sweat.

Damn, it's hot in the room. He scoots off the bed and yanks up his window, leaning against the frame as the winter wind rushes in. He closes his eyes, relishing the coolness that washes over his body.

He could leave now. He could leap right out the window and disappear before anyone ever thought to check on him again. Maybe he could go get Brett and they could disappear together. Maybe head west to California. Or south to Mexico.

He takes a long drag off the joint. God, he needs a drink. The Jack Daniel's he had hidden in here is empty, drained this afternoon.

From somewhere across the crisp air comes the sound of a passing train. He tries to picture it snaking its way across the countryside beneath the moonlight. Maybe he could hop a train and ride as far as it would go. No one would ever know what happened to him. Or why he killed them.

He quickly dresses and stuffs his backpack with a few extra clothes and the gun. He grabs his wallet; he has a little over three hundred dollars. He pulled almost everything from his savings account last month. He had intended to replace it with money he got for Christmas before Ham found out. He looks out the open door of his room. He can see Ham's legs lying in the hallway, his feet still clad in his black Rockport wing-tips. Some things are just too ironic.

Kipp grabs his jacket and heads toward the hall, toward the bodies. He stares at them for a moment. Ham's white shirt is drenched with blood and his tie is thrown crazily over his shoulder; Kipp realizes it is the paisley Mickey Mouse tie Christina gave him last Christmas. Ham's eyes are half-closed now, as if he is in ecstasy. His blood-spattered gray hair is splayed over his head like a bad wig.

Christina is virtually unrecognizable. Her eyes are still wide and shocked. The gaping hole in her head is somewhat covered by her hair, which is muddled with congealing blood, but if Kipp looks hard enough, he can see the bluish-gray of her brain. Her mouth is open, and her colorless tongue lolls between her lips. For a brief instant, Kipp considers digging out his dagger and slitting her up the front the way he fantasized about, and his dick twitches in anticipation. But there isn't time. Reluctantly, he moves past them to the darkened living room.

His eyes light on the liquor cabinet. He must have a drink. He drops his bag and his jacket and pulls out the Wild Turkey. He sips from the bottle and feels the burn down his throat, feels the warmth flow through his stomach and to the tips of his fingers and toes. He realizes he is sweating; he takes off his glasses and wipes his face on the sleeve of his shirt.

Suddenly, the room is ablaze with light through the front windows. Glancing up, he can see a car pulling into the driveway. *Shit!* He grabs his backpack and his jacket and heads toward the patio doors, toward the winter darkness outside.

4

Bruce sits in his car for a moment, not sure what to do. Lights are blazing in the bedrooms of the house, but the living room and kitchen are dark. All the cars are here. He gets out into the sharp air and trudges toward the front door. The snow on Ham's yard is old, and it crunches loudly beneath Bruce's shoes.

He rings the doorbell and stands silent. He cried all the way through town after he left Kelly's. He swipes at his eyes now, hoping they are not still red and moist. There is a jagged hole inside him now, a hole that seems to grow until it squeezes into a lump of hurt in his throat. It is a feeling he is all too familiar with.

But it will pass.

Someday, he thinks, he will have someone. He will have someone he loves and who will love him back. And it won't matter what he has done or what he has been accused of. It won't matter. And he realizes that right now, he doesn't care if it *is* a man. He doesn't care. He just needs someone to hold. Someone to love.

Impatiently, he knocks lightly on the door. He tries the knob, and the door swings open. "Ham?" he calls. "Ham, are you here?" He steps into the darkened foyer. "Hello?" He moves toward the light in the hallway, and then he sees them.

For a moment, all he can do is stare at the blood spattered and smeared on the walls. All he can feel is shocked numbness, disbelief. He turns away from the bodies, dizzied by the sight. He leans against the doorframe, gazing into nothing. He cannot fathom what he has seen. It is not real. He clenches his stomach, trying to fight the rising bile.

Stumbling, he heads for the kitchen, toward a telephone. He stops in the middle of the living room. The patio doors are open, the sheer curtains billowing in the stabbing breeze. Bruce's stomach churns in fear. He moves toward the doors, hearing his own nervous breath wheezing through his nostrils. He steps out into the cold and what he sees both relieves and terrifies him.

Kipp is standing in the middle of the dark patio, a gun pointed in front of him, pointed at Bruce. Bruce can barely see his face in the half-light. Kipp lowers the gun. "What do you want, you goddamned fuck-up?"

Bruce stares at him. "What-what happened?" he manages to blurt out. Kipp stares at him. "What happened?" he says again.

"I think they're dead," Kipp says. His voice is flat and emotionless. "I mean, I'm pretty sure they're dead."

Bruce realizes his hands have begun to shake; he shoves them into his pockets before Kipp can see. "But what *happened?*"

Kipp blows out a breath. "I shot them, you fucking moron."

Bruce can feel his knees start to wobble. "Why?" he asks, his voice quivering. "My God, what have you done?" Kipp continues to stare at him. "We've. . . we've got to call an ambulance," Bruce stammers. "We need to call somebody." He turns back toward the house.

Suddenly, he feels his hip explode in pain and his legs give way. He falls to the ice-cold concrete of the patio, and he realizes he has been shot. He looks back at Kipp. "No," he whispers. "Please, Kipp, no."

Kipp steps toward him, and Bruce jumps as the gun fires again. Hot pain sears through him. He grabs his chest and his fingers are warm and sticky with blood. "No," he says again.

He is vaguely aware of dogs barking somewhere. Next door, lights blaze on in the back yard and an angry male voice calls out. But the words make no sense. He rolls onto his back, unable to sit up.

Kipp is staring at the house next door, the gun still half-raised. Bruce can see the silver glint through the blur.

The cold of the concrete is seeping through his

clothes, stabbing into his very bones. Bruce suddenly realizes he can no longer feel his legs. And he is cold. So cold.

Kipp looks at him, then sits down on the patio. *He's watching me die*, Bruce thinks. And he wonders if this is what he did to Ham and Christina. If he watched their lives fade away, watched their last gasping, heaving moments.

Suddenly, a voice cries out behind them, "Hey, what's going on over there?" A shadow passes over them.

"Get the fuck out of here," Kipp says.

Bruce tries to lift his hand to the unseen presence. "Please," he whispers. His whole body is numb.

"Get out of here!" Kipp screams.

Bruce hears the footsteps hurrying away. He tries to reach out to Kipp. "Please," he says again.

Kipp looks at him. "Shut up and die, you piece of shit."

Bruce begins to cry again. The pain and cold are unbearable. He feels the tears pouring from his eyes, but he is powerless to wipe them away.

"Stop crying," Kipp tells him. "Stop it." He stands and gives Bruce a kick in the side of his belly, and fresh pain cuts through him. "You fat fuck," Kipp spits. He kicks again. "You big fat fuck."

Somewhere, millions of miles away, sirens wail through town. Kipp whirls around toward the sound. "Shit."

Bruce bears down against the pain. "They're coming here, Kipp," he manages to say. "You know that."

Kipp glares at him. "Shut up." He stands

motionless for a moment, listening as the sirens grow louder.

"They'll find you, you know," Bruce says. His mouth is tangy with the iron-taste of blood.

"*Shut up!*" Kipp screams, and Bruce sees that he is crying. Kipp sinks to the ground, his eyes wide and panicked. He inches the gun toward his face. He shoves the barrel beneath his chin.

Bruce tries to sit up. "No, Kipp!"

But his voice is lost in the explosion, and Kipp's lifeless form falls over onto the concrete with a sickening thud.

The sirens are growing louder each minute, but Bruce can barely hear them now. He stares straight up at the sky. There are no clouds, and through the city haze he can just see the stars. Sharp diamonds on a black velvet palette.

A strange warmth begins to spread through him, and he is no longer cold. The pain is far away. And the relief, the warmth, the peace—it is everything he has ever wanted.